Acclaim *for the* CHRISTMAS PRESENCE: THREE TALES OF LOVE

DONNA BIRDSELL

"Humor, excitement, attractive characters and a light mystery set off sparks that make *Madam of the House*, by Donna Birdsell, a great book."
—*Romantic Times BOOKreviews*

"This is her number one book. This reviewer highly recommends Ms. Birdsell's contemporary debut."
—*Loves, Romances & More*
(www.lovesromancesandmore.com) on
Suburban Secrets

LISA CHILDS

"*Learning to Hula*, by Lisa Childs, is a touching and heartwarming look at the pain of loss, leavened with laughter."
—*Romantic Times BOOKreviews*

"4-½ stars. Strong growth, not just in the heroine's life but also in her view of the people she's known forever, adds depth to the story. The hero is great, as is the growing relationship between them."
—*Romantic Times BOOKreviews* on
Taking Back Mary Ellen Black

SUSAN CROSBY

"Susan Crosby has superbly penned a tale of a man and a woman who come together to not only create a baby, but who find each other under what cannot be described as the best of terms."
—Patti Fischer, *Romance Reviews Today*

"Full of touching details… All the characters shine."
—*Romantic Times BOOKreviews* on
The Merry Widow's Diary

Donna Birdsell lives near Philadelphia, where she absolutely doesn't get any of her ideas from her perfectly normal family, friends and neighbors.

She's addicted to reality television and chocolate, loves a good snowstorm and cooks to relax.

She spent many years writing press releases, newsletters and marketing brochures until a pregnancy complication kept her home from the office. She needed something to keep her busy, so she started her very first novel.

Five years later, her dream of becoming a published fiction author came true when *The Painted Rose*, her first historical romance, was released.

You can reach Donna through her Web site at www.DonnaBirdsell.com.

Lisa Childs has been writing since she could first form sentences. At eleven she won her first writing award and was interviewed by the local newspaper. That story's plot revolved around a kidnapping, probably something she wished on any of her six siblings. A Halloween birthday predestined a life of writing intrigue. She enjoys the mix of suspense and romance.

Readers can write to Lisa at P.O. Box 139, Marne, MI 49435 or visit her at her Web site, www.lisachilds.com.

Susan Crosby believes in the value of setting goals, but also in the magic of making wishes. A longtime reader of romance novels, Susan earned a B.A. in English while raising her sons. She lives in the central valley of California, the land of wine grapes, asparagus and almonds. Her checkered past includes jobs as a synchronized swimming instructor, personnel interviewer at a toy factory and trucking company manager, but her current occupation as a writer is her all-time favorite.

Susan enjoys writing about people who take a chance on love, sometimes against all odds. She loves warm, strong heroes, good-hearted, self-reliant heroines…and happy endings.

Susan loves to hear from readers. You can visit her at her Web site, www.susancrosby.com.

THE NeXt NOVEL™

CHRISTMAS PRESENCE:
Three Tales of Love

Donna Birdsell • Lisa Childs
Susan Crosby

CHRISTMAS PRESENCE: THREE TALES OF LOVE

copyright © 2007 by Harlequin Books S.A.

isbn-13:978-0-373-88147-5

isbn-10:   0-373-88147-9

The publisher acknowledges the copyright holders of the individual
works as follows:

CHRISTMAS PRESENCE
copyright © 2007 by Donna Birdsell

SECRET SANTA
copyright © 2007 by Lisa Childs-Theeuwes

YOU'RE ALL I WANT FOR CHRISTMAS
copyright © 2007 by Susan Bova Crosby

TheNextNovel.com

 HARLEQUIN®

PRINTED IN U.S.A.

CONTENTS

CHRISTMAS PRESENCE

DONNA BIRDSELL

From the Author

Dear Reader,

I hope the season finds you happy and healthy, and looking forward to a great New Year.

Christmas has always been my favorite holiday, so when I was asked to contribute a novella to this collection, I couldn't have been more thrilled. I sat down immediately with pen and paper in hand, and roughed out the story of Astrid's *Christmas Presence*. Because the holidays seem to call to mind the people we love, I've always imagined those we've lost can't be too far away while we celebrate.

Don't forget to take some time to relax and enjoy a good book or two, to replenish that holiday spirit. And if mysterious things start happening, don't be alarmed. You just might have your own Christmas Presence….

Wishing you peace and joy,

Donna

For Ronald, Margaret, Miriam and Libby.

Hoping you are all close by.

CHAPTER 1

Tuesday, December 4, 12:30 p.m.

All she needed was a pair of panty hose.

So now here she was, in the middle of a crowded mall in the suburbs of Philadelphia, just twenty-one days before Christmas, wishing like hell she could just go to her meeting with a run in her stocking.

Because until today, Astrid Martin had almost—*almost*—managed to ignore the holidays. Aside from a few anemic decorations at the nursing home where she worked, and the occasional snippet of a Christmas song as she flipped through the channels on the radio, her exposure to all things merry had been nonexistent.

But it was kind of hard to ignore the holidays here. Fake icicles. Giant red and green Christmas balls hanging from the ceiling. Enough garland to circumnavigate the globe.

She tucked her chin into the scarf around her neck and averted her eyes, heading for the department store at the far end of the mall. Unfortunately, she didn't see the temporary kiosks that had sprung up in the middle of the promenade, and walked forehead-first into the banner of one of them, which read: Wrapping for R.U.F.F. We'll wrap anything for a buck!

"So sorry," she murmured to the two women who manned the booth. They were dressed like elves, in hats with jingle bells and red shoes that curled up at the toes.

"No problem," one of the elves said. "Hey, you look like an animal lover. Here."

The elf handed Astrid a flyer.

"Resources for Underprivileged Furry Friends (R.U.F.F.) needs you! Join our team of volunteers, and give underprivileged animals the gift of hope this Christmas."

Astrid was, in fact, an animal lover. And last year, she might have been tempted to join the R.U.F.F. volunteers in helping their furry friends. But not this year.

This year she was boycotting Christmas.

She gave the elves a polite smile, and ran away. Or rather, she tried to run away. Instead, she ran straight into a sweater.

A sweater covered in cat hair.

A sweater that covered a very broad chest, which was attached to a good-looking guy.

Easy smile. Hazelnut eyes. Hot-chocolate-brown

hair, with just a touch of marshmallow at the temples.

He bent to pick up the flyer she'd dropped when she bumped into him, and as he handed it to her he whispered, "You've got a run in your stocking."

His breath was warm in her ear, like the steam from a mug of hot cider.

Astrid tugged at her scarf. Who did this guy think he was?

Over his shoulder, she could see the elves at the wrapping booth watching them with interest. She snatched the flyer out of his hand and shoved it into her purse. "Thank you. I think."

She skirted around him and headed toward the department store, this time taking care to watch where she was going.

"Merry Christmas!" he called after her.

Right.

December 4, 3:07 p.m.

THE SOLES of Astrid's sneakers—into which she'd changed after her big meeting (at which no one even so much as glanced at her brand-new panty hose)—squeaked on the freshly waxed tiles of the third-floor hallway at Tall Pines Nursing Home.

Paper daisies pasted on the doors of the rooms, announcing the residents' names with fading cheeriness, rustled as she walked past.

Astrid stopped in front of a daisy that read VERA T.! She knocked and pushed open the door. A nurse towing a rolling blood-pressure machine was on her way out.

"Good luck," the nurse said to Astrid under her breath, "She's in rare form today."

The nurse disappeared and Astrid entered the room, closing the door behind her.

A woman for whom the adjective *birdlike* seemed to have been invented perched on the edge of an oversized armchair near the window. A lime-green-and-orange striped dress covered her slight form from neck to ankle. It looked as if it had seen better days.

The same could be said for Vera T. herself.

"Vera, how are you?" Astrid said brightly.

"How do you think I am? I can't breathe without this damned tube up my nose, I have no teeth, and I'm wearing a diaper," Vera said. "Plus we had butterscotch pudding for dessert again. Butterscotch pudding sucks."

"I know it does. But look on the bright side. At least you don't have to chew it."

After a moment of shocked silence, Vera began to squeak and wheeze. It took Astrid a second to realize she was laughing.

"Oh. Oh, dear." Vera pressed a trembling, bony finger to the corner of her eye. "I haven't laughed like that in ages."

Neither, thought Astrid, had she.

Not counting the automatic responses to sitcom gags, or the fake noises of amusement she'd perfected for her boss's corny jokes, it had been almost a year since she'd laughed. Three hundred and forty-eight days, to be exact.

"Mind if I sit down?" Astrid moved the portable oxygen tank around to the other side of Vera's recliner.

The older woman turned to face Astrid and gestured to the vinyl-padded rocking chair beside her.

"I hear you've been giving the staff a hard time," Astrid said. "Want to talk about it?"

"No." Vera frowned, and stared out the window.

Astrid waited her out. Besides the fact that the view from Vera's window wasn't great, if there was one thing she'd learned as an advocate for the elderly, it was that many of them were desperate to talk.

Or rather, they were desperate to be heard.

They had problems no one had the time, inclination or patience to deal with, and that's why Astrid was there. She listened, and tried to figure out how to make sure everyone got what they needed.

"I hate Christmas," Vera finally said. "No one gives a fart about me since Milton died."

Astrid sighed. "I know the feeling. I lost my husband, too."

Vera's sour expression mellowed. "How long has it been?"

"Eleven months, four days, six hours and—" Astrid checked her watch "—seven minutes. But who's counting?"

Actually, it seemed as if she'd been doing nothing but counting since David had died in a car accident last year. The day after Christmas.

She'd eaten breakfast alone three hundred and forty-eight times. Done *The New York Times* crossword puzzle forty-two times. Watched twenty-one episodes of *Antiques Roadshow*, gone to the movies twelve times and to the ballet twice. Alone.

This might have been her first Christmas alone, if not for the fact that she'd decided she wasn't going to *have* Christmas this year. Or maybe ever.

All the things she and David used to love—the lights, the carols, the cold. They would only serve to remind her how empty the holidays would be without him. If only she could go home, lock all the doors, and not come out until after New Year's…

She *could* survive the holidays. Hell, she could survive a nuclear attack. She still had a case of powdered milk, forty gallons of water and three cases of canned beef stew in the basement, left over from her and David's Y2K emergency plan.

Along with a cabinet full of Johnny Depp movies and an amply stocked liquor cabinet, what more could she possibly need?

Vera patted Astrid's hand, a silent message from one lonely soul to another.

Astrid smiled and leaned forward, the rocking chair creaking softly. "Vera, I want you to know you can talk to me. Tell me what you need."

Vera shook her head, sucking in a labored breath.

"No, really. Please. What can I do for you?"

Vera gave Astrid a pleading look, but said nothing.

"I know it's hard, but you can do it. You can tell me. What do you need?"

"I need…" Vera pointed toward the floor, her eyes bugging. "I need you to get your foot off my oxygen hose."

"Oh! Oh, my goodness. I'm so sorry." Astrid jumped up and pushed the rocking chair off the hose.

Vera drew in a deep breath, and broke into a coughing fit that lasted a good three minutes.

When it was over, Astrid said, "I don't think I've ever asked, but how long ago did Milton die?"

Vera rearranged her oxygen tube and settled back in her chair. "Seventeen years, nine months and twenty-two days."

Astrid shifted uncomfortably in her chair. "Wow. That's a long time."

"An eternity."

"You still miss him?"

Vera smiled. "Oh, no, dear. He's right here with me."

"You mean in your heart?"

"Why, no," Vera said. "Right here."

"In the room?"

"Of course. He talks to me all the time."

Astrid broke out in goose bumps, despite her utter disbelief in all things supernatural. "He talks to you? What does he say?"

"Oh, he pesters me like he always did. Don't you, Milton?" Vera's gaze flitted around the room. "He's always telling me what to do."

"Really? Like what?"

"He tells me what to wear. How to fix my hair. What to put on the television."

"Milton watches television?"

"Sure. He likes that MTV. Says he enjoys the music, but I think he just likes looking at the bosoms. He says Beyoncé is booty-licious."

"I see."

"He says you're not bad, either. 'Course he's always gone crazy for blondes."

Astrid hesitated. "When did he first…?"

"When did he first talk to me?" Vera said.

Astrid nodded.

"Oh, just a few weeks after he died. He just started nagging me like he never left. Been doing it ever since—what's that?" Vera cocked her head again. "Milton wants me to change the channel. There's a rerun of *Charlie's Angels* on. He likes that Farrah Fawcett."

Astrid patted Vera's hand and rose. "I'll leave the two of you alone."

December 4, 5:50 p.m.

CAPONE ATTACKED her as soon as she walked in the door.

"Jeez, can't you wait until six o'clock?"

Astrid already knew the answer to that one. A twenty-three-pound cat didn't stand on ceremony when it came to the dinner hour. Anytime after lunch could be considered supper time.

Astrid shed her coat and kicked off her shoes on the way to the cabinet where she kept the cat food. Capone pushed his dish across the kitchen floor with his forehead.

So much for the dignity of cats.

She scooped a can of Kitty Bits into Capone's dish, and it was gone before she rinsed the spoon.

"You need to go on a diet, buddy." Astrid scratched the cat's head and he hunkered down, stretching out to his full length on the linoleum. She rubbed him behind his ears until something else caught his attention and he darted off.

Astrid opened the fridge. A bottle of ketchup, half a container of yogurt and a wilted stalk of celery.

Hmm.

She checked the freezer.

The only thing that looked like it hadn't been there since the Clinton administration was a lone bean burrito.

Looked like she was going to have to go shopping if she wanted to eat. As she slipped back into her shoes and coat, Capone pounced in front of her, pushing something shiny across the floor with his paw.

"What have you got there, buddy?"

Capone lay on it.

"Come on. Move." She rolled him over, picked the thing up off the floor and examined it. "Oh, wow. Where did you find this?"

It was a little silver ring, a love knot, which David had bought for her on their first date. They'd gone to the theater in Philadelphia, and afterwards, on their way to dinner, they'd passed a street vendor selling jewelry.

David had picked this ring out and slipped it on her finger, and she'd felt an unspoken promise in the gesture. A glimpse of the future.

After the date was over, she knew she'd found her

soul mate. She'd worn the little silver ring until David had replaced it with her diamond engagement ring just three months later.

She hadn't seen it in years. Had thought she'd lost it.

She slipped it onto her finger and smiled through her tears. It was like finding an old friend.

December 4, 6:15 p.m.

THE GROCERY KING parking lot teemed with drivers who under normal circumstances would be cursing at each other, but in deference to the holiday season waited patiently for pedestrians and other cars to pass.

Hypocrites, Astrid thought, as she slogged toward the store from her parking spot miles away. At least this year *she* could feel free to be as cranky as she wanted.

And she was getting crankier by the minute, because she realized she was going to have to walk past the Christmas tree corral in the corner of the lot, where she and David used to get their tree each year.

Douglas Fir. Seven feet tall. Or was it eight? She could never remember.

But she did remember the important stuff.

Like how she and David would hold hands as they made the rounds through the corral, pretending to be walking through the woods, checking each tree twice before haggling with the salesman and then tying the one they chose to the luggage rack of the minivan, hoping it wouldn't fall off before they got home.

In the early-winter darkness, the lights strung on poles around the corral twinkled merrily. "White Christmas" drifted out over the lot, Bing Crosby's smooth vocals slowing Astrid's stride.

She breathed deeply, the pungent smell of evergreen filling her nose. Evergreen mixed with the scent of something else. Something familiar. Comforting.

David's cologne.

Astrid stopped in the middle of the parking lot, and closed her eyes.

It was as if he were there right at that moment, with her. Thinking about the tree, and the lights, and "White Christmas." Taking her hand…

Her fingers curled, but came up empty.

Beeeeeeeep.

"Hey, lady. You gonna move or what?" The guy hung out the driver's-side window of a green sedan, making rude hand gestures.

So much for hypocritical politeness.

Astrid brushed a tear from her cheek and hurried toward the automatic doors of the Grocery King, feeling like an ass.

It had been proven that the sense of smell was the most powerful of the senses in evoking memories. In fact, she'd used it many times in her work with elderly clients to elevate mood, stimulate appetite and prompt memories of youth.

Memories of better times. Phantom memories, like missing limbs.

The automatic doors of the store slid open and Astrid hurried out of the cold and into the produce department. She didn't like cooking, but she always found grocery stores comforting. Probably because she liked to eat.

She picked up a grapefruit—the thirty-sixth since David died. They used to share them, half and half.

She put it in her cart, averting her eyes as she passed a stand of poinsettias. And a display of candy canes. And a giant cardboard Santa holding a tube of hemorrhoid cream, presumably because riding a sleigh around the entire world in one night was torture on his tender backside.

She was doing so well avoiding Christmas, she didn't see the Martha Stewart look-alike holding a tray of eggnog samples who ambushed her in the dairy aisle.

"Taste?" The woman held out a tiny cup of the yellow, viscous liquid.

"No, thanks." Astrid tried to sidle around her, but the woman was having none of it.

"Little taste?" She pushed the cup toward Astrid.

"No, thank you. I don't care for eggnog."

"Please," the woman muttered under her breath, through a clenched smile. "Just take it. My boss is watching. You want to get me fired? I got three grandchildren who all want a Silly Sally doll for Christmas. Do you know how much those suckers are going for on eBay? I need this job."

"All right. No problem." Astrid took the little cup and started to walk away.

"Drink it."

Astrid turned, startled. "What?"

"You have to drink it. And make it look like you enjoy it. Please?"

"Wow. Okay. Right." Astrid held her breath and knocked back the eggnog like a shot of tequila. She put the little paper cup back on the tray, and wiped her mouth with the back of her hand. "Well, thank you. Good luck."

She turned her gimpy cart toward the deli section, trying hard to keep from throwing up. She really couldn't stand eggnog.

From halfway down the aisle, the sample lady called out to her. "Hey, wait! I get a commission for every quart I sell!"

A FEW MINUTES later, Astrid trudged toward her car, her arms already aching from the weight of the grocery bags she carried.

As she passed the tree corral, "Silver Bells" played on the speaker system. David's favorite Christmas song.

She stole a glance at the lights twinkling against the black of the night sky like nearby stars. From between the trees leaned up against the makeshift fence, a movement caught her eye.

A Russian-style hat with faux-fur earflaps bobbed amongst the branches. It was a horrible hat. Ridiculous, really. And…

The hair on the back of her neck stood up…

It was exactly like the one David had worn the first time they'd come for a tree.

And the cologne. His cologne again! She could smell it.

And then a voice, whispering to her.

David?

No, no! This was crazy. It was the wind through the tree branches, or her mind playing tricks. Or—

Vera Tait.

Maybe David was talking to her like Milton Tait talked to Vera.

Okay, Astrid. Get a grip. Vera Tait is off her rocker. There are no such things as ghosts—

A whiff of cologne. Another whisper…

She *did* hear him! She'd heard him as clearly as she'd heard the guy in the sedan swearing at her. And he'd said, "Get a tree."

"David?" Astrid's arms gave out and the grocery

bags plummeted to the macadam, the contents spilling out. Eggnog pooled at her feet.

Get a tree?

Under no circumstances would she get a tree.

A tree would be hard to carry. It would make a mess in the house. But most importantly, a tree would go against everything she was trying to accomplish this holiday season.

A tree would make it pretty hard to ignore Christmas.

CHAPTER 2

December 4, 11:30 p.m.

Astrid hung one last ornament on the tree and stepped back to survey her work. "What do you think, Capone? How does it look?"

Capone growled the way only a twenty-three-pound tabby can growl, and threaded his corpulent body around Astrid's calves, leaving wads of yellow cat fur on Astrid's black pants.

"I'll assume you approve."

So did she. Sort of.

Despite the fact that she'd overestimated the size of tree she needed, and had to lop a foot off the top before she and the neighbor's kid could stand it up, and then she hadn't been able to reach high enough to decorate the uppermost branches, it looked pretty good.

For the life of her, she couldn't figure out what had possessed her to buy it. She'd gone into the tree corral to look for the man with the hat like David's, but never did find him, and she'd pretty much convinced herself she was temporarily insane. Then somehow she'd ended up with a tree tied to the roof of the minivan. Just like old times. Almost.

"This is for you, David," she whispered, as she turned on the tree lights with a remote control. This would be her one concession to Christmas.

She knelt down beside the tree and collected a few stray ornaments she'd decided not to hang, grabbing some paper from the recycling basket to wrap them before putting them back in the box.

She unfolded a piece and laid it out on the floor, but before she could use it, Capone flopped down in the middle of it.

"Come on, move it, buddy." She elbowed the cat, but he wouldn't budge. He slapped the paper with his paw.

"No no. We're not playing right now. Get off the paper."

Capone looked up at her and slapped the paper again. Just below his paw, it read, "Wrapping for R.U.F.F."

The flyer the elves had given her at the mall.

Astrid grabbed a corner of the paper and pulled it free from Capone's generous hind end.

"Raaawr." Capone rolled over onto his back and stared up at her. He looked almost as if he was trying to tell her something.

Do it.

If she hadn't been looking right at him, she would have sworn Capone had talked to her. But it wasn't him.

The hair on the back of her neck stood up.

"David?"

Gooseflesh broke out on her arms. Now she was just creeping herself out.

"Stop it, Astrid," she said to herself. "You're being ridiculous. David *cannot* talk to you."

She shook off the feeling she wasn't alone and packed up the ornaments she hadn't used.

She set the box near the steps to take up to the attic later, and went to the kitchen to make some tea.

She'd never been one of those people who believed in signs or omens or whispering ghosts, but when she got to the kitchen she stopped short. The goose bumps returned with a vengeance.

Something strange was going on. Something very, very strange.

A piece of paper lay on the table. The same piece of paper she'd just used to wrap a porcelain Santa ornament. The R.U.F.F. flyer.

Do it.

"What? What do you want me to do?"

Silence.

She picked up the flyer. "David? Do you want me to volunteer for that booth? Is that what you're saying?"

Capone padded into the kitchen and sat at her feet, purring like a misfiring engine. Astrid looked down at him, and she could have sworn he was smiling.

Do it.

"Oh, no. No way. The tree was one thing, but I can't sit there in the middle of the mall during the holiday season, with the Christmas music and the people and the gifts."

"Reooow," Capone said.

"No way, David. You hear me? *No way.*"

Thursday, December 6, 5:57 p.m.

ASTRID SLID her feet into the pointed elf shoes that came with the rest of the ridiculous elf outfit. "This is it," she muttered under her breath. "This is the last Christmasy thing I do." She stuffed her clothes into a plastic bag and marched out of the restroom, into the expansive, marble-floored corridor of the Bridgeton Mall.

The place was wall-to-wall Christmas. Greens and wide red ribbons climbed every column. Storefronts sported posters announcing spectacular sales. An overworked Santa juggled crying kids while "Jingle Bells" blared from the sound system.

Astrid focused on the wrapping booth, pushing her way past a long line of shoppers laden with bags of what she assumed were gifts to be wrapped. Her coworkers for the evening were already there, dressed in the same asinine outfit as she was, looking frazzled and desperate.

"I'm Edith," said an older woman with tight, gray curls and drawn-on eyebrows. Astrid recognized her as the woman who'd handed her the flyer that got her into this mess. "And this is Carla. We're supposed to show you the ropes."

Astrid squeezed into the booth beside Carla, a compact, fifty-something lady with an overbite and at least a thousand freckles. She stuffed the bag with her clothes beneath the hard plastic chair that would serve as her private hell for the next three hours.

"Are we the only volunteers tonight?" Astrid asked.

"Honey, we're the only volunteers period," Carla said. "It hasn't been a great season for R.U.F.F."

Edith pointed out the industrial-sized rolls of wrapping paper, ribbon and tape, and Carla handed Astrid a cash box for the money she'd collect.

"A buck a gift," Edith said. "And we wrap anything. Nothing too big or too small." She ducked past Carla, plopped into her chair and left Astrid to fend for herself.

The line at the booth divided like an amoeba, and instantly Astrid had a dozen people waiting to have their gifts professionally wrapped by a woman who was boycotting Christmas.

The first customer up, a lady with hair the color of a stop sign and lipstick to match, dropped her gift onto the wrapping table with a thud.

Astrid eyed it skeptically. "You want me to wrap *that?*"

"Yes."

"A bowling ball?"

"Uh-huh."

"You're kidding, right?"

"Of course I'm not kidding. The sign says you'll wrap anything for a dollar."

Edith flashed Astrid a look, and mouthed the word *anything*.

Astrid sighed, and tore a piece of wrapping paper off the roll.

It was going to be a long night.

December 6, 8:45 p.m.

AS IT TURNED OUT, the bowling ball was only the first, and most definitely not the worst, of the odd-shaped—and just plain odd—gifts Astrid was asked to wrap.

A musical toilet seat…a naked garden gnome…a bacon-scented candle…a fishing rod…and the coup de grâce, a stuffed trout.

A stuffed trout? For crying out loud, didn't anyone give nice, normal gifts anymore?

David had always given her nice gifts. Thoughtful gifts that meant something. Last Christmas he'd given her a lovely antique vase. Inside it he'd left a note saying he'd hired a professional landscaper to help her plan her dream garden in the backyard, so she could fill the vase with flowers.

Astrid's throat constricted.

She'd cancelled the landscaper. She couldn't imagine creating something beautiful without having David to share it with her.

"Hey, lady. You're crying all over my trout."

"Sorry." Astrid sniffed, and pasted a bow on the so-called gift.

The guy grabbed his fish, threw a dollar bill at her and took off, no doubt terrified at the prospect of having to console a weeping elf.

Astrid squeezed her eyes shut, willing herself to pull it together. Nineteen more days and Christmas would be over. Twenty, and she'd pass the anniversary of David's death.

"Excuse me, miss? Are you okay?"

She opened her eyes.

Cat hair on a sweater.

A different sweater, but most definitely the same guy. Mr. Hot-Cocoa-and-Marshmallows Hair. Mr.

Hazelnut Eyes. The guy she'd run into—literally—when she was buying panty hose on Tuesday.

Now that she had a chance to really look at him, she noticed he was a little older than she'd thought. And much better-looking.

His eyes, flecked with gold, she saw now, were kind. His smile was comforting.

And expectant.

"I'm sorry, sir. What would you like me to wrap?"

He held out a long, narrow box.

She took it and he said, "Would you mind telling me what you think? Give me a woman's opinion?"

"Sure." She had an irrational hope that it wasn't a flashing tie or fake dreadlocks.

She opened the box to reveal a gorgeous hand-painted silk scarf. Astrid skimmed a finger over the delicate rendering of a dragonfly.

"Beautiful," she said. "You have good taste."

His cheeks flushed an appealing shade of red. "Thanks."

Astrid closed the box and chose a poinsettia-print paper to wrap the scarf, finishing it with a tasteful gold ribbon and bow.

He offered her a dollar, but when she tried to take it he held on to it until her eyes met his.

"What's your name?" he said.

Astrid was momentarily taken aback. "I— It's Astrid."

"Nice to meet you, Astrid. My name is Blake."

"Well, Blake, may I have the dollar?"

His cheeks flushed again. "Of course."

He shuffled around in front of the table as she stuck his dollar bill in the cashbox.

"Astrid," he said. "That's an unusual name. Very pretty."

"Thank you."

Good lord, was he hitting on her? Wow. Of all the experiences she didn't want to count right now, that one was at the top of her list. Right above Christmas.

"Astrid, would you like to—"

She cleared her throat. "Will that be all, then? I really should take care of these other people."

She looked beyond him, to…

Nobody.

Where had everyone gone? Where were the half dozen people who'd just been behind him, with their elephant-feet slippers and tacky jewelry and talking cookie jars?

Suddenly they had disappeared, and Edith and Carla were gathering up their things to leave, too.

"Booth's closing," Edith said. "I'll take your cashbox." She gave Blake a sideways glance, winked at Astrid and then she and Carla disappeared, too.

Blake gave Astrid a nervous smile. "If you're finished here, would you like to go have a cup of coffee with me?"

"Oh…" She looked at her watch. "I'm sorry, I really can't. I've got an early day tomorrow."

"Sure. Of course." Blake tucked the present under his arm. "Maybe some other time?"

Astrid gave a noncommittal head bob and said, "Thanks for supporting R.U.F.F."

"Pardon me?"

"R.U.F.F." She pointed to the banner across the top of the booth.

"Oh, right." He smiled. "See you around."

Or not.

Because she was never, ever going to work in this booth again.

CHAPTER 3

Saturday, December 8, 8:55 a.m.

"G'morning." Edith waved to Astrid, who shoved her plastic bag full of clothes under her chair. Again.

"You look like you could use a cup of coffee," Carla said.

"No kidding."

It had been a terrible night.

Astrid had lain in bed—which still felt lonely after two thousand and fifty-eight hours of sleeping without David—"Deck the Halls" playing over and over in her mind. At least she'd thought it was in her mind, until it occurred to her it could be coming from elsewhere.

Like the attic.

Sometime around midnight she'd slipped into her robe and gone up there, and sure enough, she'd found the source of the song. A music box David had given her their first Christmas together, buried at the bottom of a box of holiday decorations. She figured she must have disturbed the box when she'd put the tree ornaments back in the attic.

She'd held the music box in her hand as it played itself out, then gently closed the lid and returned it to the box of decorations. She scrambled down out of the freezing-cold attic, tired and shaken, wanting only to curl up under the covers and fall asleep.

But as soon as she'd climbed back into bed, she heard the music again. It wouldn't stop. Wouldn't wind down. And that's when she knew that David was sending her another message, and this time she didn't even have to hear his voice to know what it was.

He wanted her to put up the Christmas decorations.

She put her pillow over her head, but she could still hear the music. Then she'd stuffed cotton in her ears, but she could still hear the music.

So finally she'd tumbled wearily out of bed and made her way back up to the attic, collected all the boxes of decorations, and spent the better part of the night decking the halls. The last thing she did was put the music box on the mantel and wind it up to play.

She'd fallen asleep facedown in a pile of garland, and was awakened at the crack of dawn by Capone, who chewed on her earlobe in a not-so-subtle appeal for his breakfast. She'd dragged herself into the kitchen, turned on the local TV station, and seen a shot of the R.U.F.F. booth at the mall. The picture froze, as if the television station was having technical difficulties, but she knew better.

It was David. Again.

"Reeeeooww," Capone said.

Astrid shook her head in defeat. "All right. I get it."

So here she was at the mall at nine o'clock on a Saturday morning, two weeks and two days before Christmas. The last place on earth she wanted to be.

"You better wake up, honey," Edith said, handing her a doughnut. "It's gonna be a crazy day."

That turned out to be a gross understatement.

By noon, Astrid had wrapped a plaster penguin, a pith helmet, a traffic cone, an Elvis clock with swinging hips, a pair of Lucite shoes and a lawn flamingo.

She was just about to take her lunch break when Blake appeared. He stood at the back of Astrid's line, even though Edith's and Carla's were much shorter.

He wore a tan jacket with a black turtleneck underneath, and as he moved closer Astrid could see the cat hair on it. Blake's gaze met hers, and he smiled.

Astrid suddenly felt warm. "Is it getting hot in here?"

Edith's gaze followed hers, and she whistled. "It sure is."

Astrid fumbled with the skateboard she was wrapping. The wheels kept poking through the paper. "Arrgh! Edith, do you mind if I take my lunch break now?"

"Don't you want to wait until that hunky guy makes it to the booth? I think he's interested."

"Well, I'm not." It came out a lot sharper than Astrid intended, and Edith gave her a wounded look.

Astrid sighed. "I'm sorry, Edith. I just… I'm just not in the market to meet anyone."

"Pity," Edith said, staring at Blake. "If I were younger, I'd go for it in a heartbeat. That guy is melting the candy bar in my pocket."

"What about Harvey?" Carla said.

"Who?" said Edith.

"Your husband. Harvey."

"Oh, yeah. Harvey." Edith sighed, and returned her attention to the package she was wrapping. "Well, if you want to have lunch, go ahead, Astrid. I just think it's a shame to waste an opportunity like that one. If I were you, *I'd* be in the market. Especially if I could shop for something *that* delicious."

Astrid stole one more glance at Blake, and then ducked out the back of the booth. She definitely was *not* in the market.

Not even for something that delicious.

December 8, 12:50 p.m.

AFTER A SALAD and a quick cry in the ladies' room, Astrid elbowed her way back to the wrapping booth, steeling herself for another two hours and ten minutes of ungodly Christmas gifts and annoying holiday cheer.

Why would David torture her like this?

She slid back into the booth and shoved her handbag under her chair beside the plastic bag containing her street clothes. When she looked up, she nearly fell off her chair.

Blake was at the back of the line. Again.

Astrid shook her head. "I don't believe it."

"He's been waiting for you to come back," Edith said with a grin.

"Great."

She plodded through a deluge of gifts, her nervous fingers struggling with the tape and ribbon, until Blake stepped up to the counter.

"Hi," he said. "Remember me?"

"Weren't you in line earlier?"

"I was. But I skipped out."

"Why?"

He shrugged. "I wanted to wait for you. You did such a great job with the scarf yesterday."

He unloaded the contents of the shopping bag he carried onto the counter.

Toys.

A doll, a fire truck, Lincoln Logs.

He had children. Young children.

Astrid was surprised. Blake wasn't old, maybe a

few years older than she, but he still didn't look quite young enough to have children this small.

Tears stung the backs of her eyelids.

She and David had spent the first decade of their marriage traveling, eating in five-star restaurants, and remodeling their home, content in each others' company. By the time they'd gotten around to talking about having children, it was too late.

Astrid was already in her forties, and fertility tests showed that it would take a lot of medical intervention that might not even be successful in the end. So they'd decided not to pursue it.

It was one of Astrid's deepest regrets.

She wrapped Blake's gifts quickly and efficiently, and placed them back in the shopping bag. "That'll be three dollars, please."

Blake pulled a wallet out of the back pocket of his jeans, and took out three dollar bills.

"How about that coffee?" he said.

Astrid shook her head. "Thanks for the offer, but no."

"I had a feeling you'd say that." Blake picked up his shopping bag and gave her a resigned smile. "Have a nice afternoon, Astrid."

As he walked away, Edith looked at Astrid and shook her head. "You're crazy."

Astrid thought about all the time she'd been

spending taking orders from David's ghost, and thought that Edith might have a point.

Friday, December 14, 4:49 p.m.

MAYBE IT WAS the passing of the full moon, or too many sugary treats going around. Whatever the reason, Tall Pines seemed more like an asylum than a nursing home that week.

On Monday, Mr. Cappiletti and Mr. Sanporo ran a drag race on their electric scooters down the mail hall, in an ongoing grudge match that had started the previous summer at the Yahtzee tournament.

On Tuesday, Mrs. Getz declared a hunger strike until the brand of laundry detergent was changed. Wednesday Mr. Danehoffer decided to microwave his false teeth, and on Thursday afternoon, Mrs. Kruger took a skinny dip in the lobby fountain.

By the end of the day on Friday, Astrid wanted nothing more than to go home, pour a glass of wine and soak in a hot tub. But she had one more stop to make before she could leave.

Vera Tait sat in her chair by the window, brooding again, when Astrid walked into her room.

"How are you today, Vera?" Astrid set the grocery bag she carried down on the bed tray and unloaded one container each of chocolate, rice and tapioca pudding onto the tray. The sight of the pudding coaxed a smile to Vera's lips.

"I'll put these in your little fridge," Astrid said. "Just in case the dining room decides to serve butterscotch again."

"Thank you," the older woman said. "And Milton says thank you, too. He's happy I've found a friend."

Astrid smiled, and took Vera's hand in hers. "I'm happy, too."

Vera ran a finger over Astrid's ring. The love knot. Astrid hadn't taken it off since Capone had found it.

"Pretty," said Vera.

"David gave it to me on our first date." Astrid drew her hand away and studied the ring. "I guess I've felt closer to him since I put it on."

Vera leaned in and whispered conspiratorially, "Has he talked to you?"

Astrid didn't say anything.

"That's when my Milton started talking to me, you know. When I put this necklace on." She reached into the neck of her blouse and showed Astrid a gold heart pendant.

"He started talking to you because of that?"

Could it really be the ring? Astrid rubbed it unconsciously.

Vera nodded, as if there was no need to elaborate. "You'll get used to it."

Would she?

For as much as she missed David, she was getting awfully tired of acting on his little whims. The tree, the decorations, the wrapping booth. A couple of days ago he had her sending out Christmas cards, a job that was his when he was alive.

She couldn't figure out why David was so insistent that she get into the Christmas spirit. She just couldn't.

All the trappings might be there—the tinsel and mistletoe and music—but her heart just wasn't in it. And however close David's spirit might be, it wasn't the same as being with *him*.

"What's that?" Vera suddenly said. She cocked her head to the left. "Milton asked if you would turn on the television. *Baywatch* is coming on."

Astrid smiled. "Of course."

She supposed she should be grateful that David was into Christmas instead of boobs.

CHAPTER 4

December 14, 7:00 p.m.

Astrid hated to admit it, but it was nice to come home to the fresh scent of pine. Though she supposed she could have gotten that just by opening a bottle of Pine Sol.

She kicked off her shoes, dropped her bag near the front door and headed for the kitchen and the glass of cabernet she'd been fantasizing about since late that afternoon.

Okay, *early* that afternoon.

Okay, early that *week*.

She felt the air shift and closed her eyes, waiting. Nothing happened. She pressed the wineglass to her forehead. "Astrid, you really are losing it."

No more thinking about ghosts. No more imagining David was here with her, telling her what to do. That might be okay for lonely old women like Vera Tait, but it wasn't okay for *her*.

She had to face facts. David was gone.

It was okay to be alone. It sucked, but it wasn't going to kill her.

"The thing is, Capone," she said, "sometimes I really feel him here. You know?"

Capone blinked.

Astrid headed for the living room. On the way past the bookshelves where she kept her cookbooks, she noticed that the spine of one of them was sticking out. She pushed it with her knee, but it wouldn't budge.

She set down the wine and pushed the book with her hands, but it wouldn't go back in. So she pulled it out.

The corner of a photograph stuck out from the top. She opened the cookbook, and David's face smiled up at her from between the pages.

The photo had been taken five or six years before, on a Christmas ski trip to Lake Placid. David's face was ruddy with windburn, his blue eyes bright. Whiteface Mountain rose up behind him, covered in a bright white blanket of snow.

The bed-and-breakfast where they had stayed had served the most marvelous Christmas cookies, which prompted Astrid's purchase of this very cookbook. She'd made the cookies every year since. They were one of only a handful of recipes she made that ever came out right.

She tucked the picture in between the pages of

the cookbook and slid it back into its place on the shelf. Capone rubbed up against her legs.

"Meeowwwl." He jumped up onto the bookshelves and pawed at the cookbook she'd just replaced. It fell off the shelf and opened to the page she'd just been looking at. David stared up at her, smiling.

She looked at Capone. "What are you? David's henchman?"

Capone purred and pawed at the book.

Astrid expelled a breath. "I guess I'm making cookies."

Saturday, December 15, 12:20 a.m.

THREE-QUARTERS of a bottle of wine and nine dozen cookies later, Astrid stuck the last cookie sheet in the dishwasher and dried her hands on her pants.

She gave Capone a dirty look. "What am I supposed to do with all these cookies?"

Capone licked his chops.

"No way. You're fat enough." Astrid picked up a cookie and took a bite. "And I will be, too, if I eat all of these."

She threw the half-eaten cookie in the trash can and picked up her wine. "Is it okay if I go to bed now, David?"

Nothing. Even Capone was silent.

She turned off the kitchen light.

* * *

December 15, 9:30 a.m.

"Mmm. These are good." Edith and Carla munched on the cookies Astrid had brought to the wrapping booth.

"Glad you like them."

Astrid yawned and pasted a bow on a personal lie detector from the Electronics Hut. The gift that would keep on giving.

"I thought you said you weren't going to celebrate Christmas this year," Edith said, brushing crumbs off her green-and-white-striped elf pants.

Astrid shrugged. "What can I say? I was overcome by a Christmas spirit."

"Don't you mean *the* Christmas spirit?" Carla said.

"Whatever." Astrid motioned for the next person in line. Great. A rake. How in the hell was she going to wrap a rake?

As she worked, she found herself surreptitiously searching the line for Blake's now-familiar face. She couldn't say why, exactly. Maybe because his gifts were practically the only normal ones she'd wrapped since she'd started this job.

Around two o'clock, just before her shift ended, he appeared. She caught him peering at her from behind a large man in a dark green parka.

When he reached her, she couldn't help but smile.

"Were you hiding behind that guy?"

Blake shrugged. "I guess I was. I was afraid you'd disappear if you saw me coming." He set a box on the table and opened it, revealing a hand-blown glass bowl decorated with dragonflies.

She nodded her approval, and set about wrapping it.

"How's everything going?" he asked. He sounded genuinely curious. Maybe even concerned?

"Do I look that bad?" she said.

"No! No, you look good. A little tired, maybe."

"I was up late."

"Hot date?"

"Yeah. With my oven." She reached under the table and pulled out the container of cookies she'd brought. "Would you like one?"

"Sure."

He pored over the cookies, choosing a delicate little pecan tassie. David's favorite.

Blake bit into the tender center of the tiny cake, and closed his eyes. "Mmm. I haven't tasted anything like this since… Well, for quite a while."

"That's good, I hope."

"Very good. But you know what would go great with this cookie?"

"What?" She tied a ribbon around the box.

"Coffee."

"Hmm."

"And you know what would go good with coffee?"

"What?"

"A conversation with you."

"Blake—"

"It's just coffee, Astrid. Coffee and conversation. You're not going to turn me down again, are you? I don't think my ego could take it."

Beside her, Astrid could see Carla hanging on Blake's words. Edith kicked Astrid under the table.

"All right! I mean, yes. I'll have coffee with you," she said.

Blake smiled. Wow. He had a fantastic smile.

"Great. When do you get out of that booth?"

Astrid checked her watch. "In about forty-five minutes."

"How about you meet me upstairs at the coffee place in the food court?"

"Okay." She handed him the box she'd wrapped and he tucked it under his arm.

He gave her a dollar, and slung his jacket over his shoulder. "I'll see you soon."

She wanted to call after him. Tell him she'd made a huge mistake. But the view as he walked away left her just a little bit speechless.

December 15, 3:00 p.m.

BY THE TIME her shift was over, Astrid had considered and reconsidered Blake's offer a dozen times.

And she'd decided it had been a rash decision to agree to meet him.

She was tired. Delirious, actually. Not thinking straight at all. She just wanted to go home and take a nap.

Fortunately, the food court was at the opposite end of the mall on the second floor, so she'd have no problem ducking out without running into Blake.

She rooted around under her chair for the bag containing her street clothes, but couldn't find it. After ten minutes searching the booth, she was forced to conclude that the bag was gone. She was going to have to drive home in her elf costume.

She grabbed her handbag, which by some miracle was still there, and slung it over her shoulder. She said goodbye to Edith and Carla and headed for the door to the parking lot, happy to have a legitimate excuse for skipping out on Blake.

The bells on her elf slippers jingling, she drew snickers from a group of boys hanging outside the mall entrance, texting messages on their cell phones, flipping skateboards and drinking sodas from giant plastic cups.

She wondered if their parents knew what they were doing.

And then she wondered when she'd gotten old enough to have *that* thought.

At the van, she dug through her handbag for her

keys. When she couldn't find them, she dumped the entire contents of her purse onto the hood.

No keys.

She peered into the passenger-side window, and saw her keys dangling from the ignition.

Unbelievable.

In the mess on her hood, she found the card with the phone number for AAA, but no cell phone. She looked into the car again, and sure enough there it was, tucked in the drink holder on the center console.

"Great. Just great," she muttered under her breath.

Well, she was just going to have to find a phone.

She shoved everything into her purse and trudged back toward the mall, stopping when she reached the kids at the entrance.

"Hey, can I borrow your phone?" she asked one of the boys. "I locked my keys in the car."

The kid smirked at her. "Don't you mean your sleigh?"

His buddies laughed.

"Hey," said another one. "Weren't you in *Lord of the Rings?*"

"Very funny. Now, can I borrow someone's phone?"

A kid with pants so baggy they hung halfway

down his thighs said, "Who you calling? Santa Claus?"

"As a matter of fact, yes. I'm going to tell him to bring you a belt for Christmas. And a book on how to get a girlfriend."

"Yo, how do you know I don't already *have* a girlfriend?" He struck a gangsta pose.

Astrid said, "Because if you did have a girlfriend, you wouldn't be hanging out in front of the mall with a bunch of *guys*."

"Busted, dude!" said one of his friends. They all laughed.

The kid's face turned red. "Here."

Astrid took his phone and dialed AAA. The customer service rep told her it would be at least ninety minutes until they could have someone there.

She gave the rep a description of her van and where it was parked before handing the phone back to the kid. "Thanks."

He grinned. "Tell Rudolph I said hi."

"Sure thing." She jingled back into the mall.

What was she going to do for the next hour and a half? It wasn't as if she could blend in to the crowd and do a little shopping. She needed somewhere to hide out.

And maybe a cup of coffee while she was doing it.

CHAPTER 5

December 15, 3:35 p.m.

Blake was sitting at a small table for two in the far corner of the coffee place, anxiously watching the door. He seemed both relieved and disconcerted when Astrid arrived.

He stood and pulled the other chair out for her. Astrid hesitated before she sat.

"Sorry I'm late. I…ah…I lost my clothes."

Blake jingled one of the bells on her collar with his finger. "I don't think I've ever had coffee with an elf before. A leprechaun, yes. A fairy, yes. But never an elf."

"I guess there's a first time for everything."

Like this. Her first time having coffee with a man since her husband died.

Her first time having coffee with a man other than her husband in sixteen years.

Oh, God. She just wanted to turn around and run out of there as fast as her elf shoes could take her.

But the way Blake was looking at her, as if he was just as nervous—and every bit as vulnerable—as she was, made her plant herself in the seat.

It's only coffee, she told herself.

"What would you like?" Blake asked.

"How about a cappuccino?"

"You want cinnamon on it?"

"Sure, why not?"

He placed their order and watched her uneasily from the counter, as if he were afraid she'd disappear into thin air.

"Here you go," he said when he returned. He set a giant paper cup in front of her. "I thought you might like this, too."

Almond biscotti, half dipped in chocolate.

"Biscotti is one of my all-time favorite things," she said. "You must be psychic."

"Something like that." He sat down across from her and blew the steam off the top of his own coffee.

Black, she noticed. Nothing fancy.

"So."

"So." She sipped her cappuccino.

"Is it okay?" he asked.

"To tell you the truth, I've never had cappuccino before."

He smiled. "Why did you order it?"

She shrugged. "I guess it's a day for new things. Generally, I prefer tea over coffee."

He gave her a strange look. "Yes. Right. I should have known that."

"How could you possibly?"

"I don't. I mean, I wouldn't, right?" He stared down at his coffee for a moment, as if he were embarrassed. Then he said, "Tell me something else about you."

She stirred her cappuccino with a wooden stick, swirling the cinnamon into the steamed milk. "Well, I'm not really an elf."

He laughed. "Go on."

"I'm…" She sighed. "I'm actually a widow. A rather new one. And I'm having a really difficult time dealing with the holidays, and I thought this might be a good idea, but I'm feeling a little guilty right now—"

She stood.

"Please, don't go." Blake reached up and touched her elbow. "I know how you feel. I'm a widower. Lost my wife four and a half years ago. I hate the holidays, too."

"Really? I'm sorry." Astrid sank back into her chair.

"I'm sorry, too. She was a wonderful woman."

"Have you…" Astrid stared into her coffee. "Have you dated much?"

Blake shook his head. "Not much. I've always felt like I'm betraying her."

"I feel that way right now," Astrid said. She touched the love-knot ring, and took a split second to see if she could feel David staring down at her from above. If she could feel his disappointment. But all she felt was a mild caffeine rush.

Blake touched her arm. "How about if we don't call this a date? I think we could both use a friend right now. Someone who knows what we're going through."

She nodded, relieved.

"Good. Can I get you another biscotti?"

For the next hour they talked. About everything. About Blake's wife, Christine, who'd died of cancer. About David's accident the day after Christmas, when he'd been simply driving around the corner for milk.

About Blake's children and grandchildren, and their upcoming Christmas visit. About art and music and the best way to fertilize rosebushes.

The next time Astrid looked at her watch, it was time for her to get back to her car to meet the AAA mechanic.

"I have to go," she said, picking up the napkins and stir sticks and sugar packets that littered their table. "But thank you. I had a very nice time talking with you."

Blake smiled. Genuine, without the uneasiness he'd shown earlier. "Me, too. Can we do it again sometime?"

Astrid could detect no hint of salaciousness. No trace of anything other than comfortable camaraderie. She felt as if she'd be safe in Blake's company. And so would her memory of David.

"I'd like that," she said. "I'd like that a lot."

Monday, December 17, 9:10 a.m.

AN UNEXPECTED spate of tears—her one hundred and seventy-second—made Astrid late for work.

It was silly, really. But when she'd been looking through the mail basket for a stamp, she'd found a receipt from last December for one of David's Christmas gifts. The last thing she'd ever bought him.

Socks.

She sobbed. How could she have ever been so unromantic? So ordinary? Poor David.

She complained about the gifts she'd wrapped at the R.U.F.F. booth, and meanwhile she'd been no better herself. *Socks!*

She carefully folded the receipt and tucked it back into the basket, unable to throw it away. Then she drove to work in a fog, trying to remember if David had been wearing those socks the day he died.

When she arrived at Tall Pines, she dumped her briefcase on her desk and leafed through her interoffice mail. In it was a message from the staff physician. She read the note, and headed directly up to the third floor.

"How's Vera Tait?" she asked one of the nurses.

"As well as can be expected," the other woman said. "It won't be long, I'm afraid."

Astrid nodded. "Has anyone made arrangements for hospice care?"

"No. I don't think she's got a soul in the world to do it, so Psychological Services is going to take care of it."

"I'll do it," Astrid said. "Will you make a copy of her chart and send it down to me?"

"Sure."

Astrid grabbed a fresh cup of ice water and a straw from the kitchenette behind the nurse's station and headed to Vera's room.

The older woman was lying in her bed, covered with an old patchwork quilt, staring at the ceiling. Astrid set the cup of water on the rolling tray beside the bed and took Vera's bony hand in hers.

"How are you feeling today?"

Vera was silent.

"Mrs. T? Can you hear me?"

"Just a minute. I'm listening to Milton."

Astrid sat quietly until Vera rolled over onto her side.

"I have cancer. I'm dying, you know."

Astrid swallowed. "Yes, I got a copy of the doctor's report. I'm so sorry, Vera."

Vera shrugged. "What can you do? I'm old. Something was bound to get me."

"Is there anyone you'd like me to contact? Any children?"

Vera shook her head. "Milton and I traveled a lot for his job, and back in those days it wasn't so easy bringing children along. No disposable diapers and baby carriers and such. Besides, we just always thought we'd have each other."

"What about siblings? Anybody?"

"I have a cousin out in Barstow, Minnesota. Name's Anne Pritchard. We haven't spoken in a while, though."

"Would you like me to contact her for you?"

Vera shrugged. "No sense in it now. Dying is a lonely business." She stared out the window. "I guess living is, too. Isn't it?"

Astrid squeezed her hand. "Sometimes it is."

"You know, right after he died, Milton told me never to find anyone else. Said he wouldn't be able to stand it if I did. Said it would kill him all over again."

"Really?"

Vera nodded. "So I didn't. And let me tell you, lots of men asked. I was pretty good-looking back then. But I couldn't do it to Milton. Not knowing he was still with me."

"Of course."

"Sometimes I didn't want to listen, though. You know?"

Astrid nodded. "I know."

"But I'm glad I did," said Vera, her voice fading. "I'm glad I did."

December 17, 6:15 p.m.

ASTRID ARRIVED home in much the same condition in which she'd left that morning. Her conversation with Vera Tait had left her rattled. Weepy.

She slogged into the kitchen and listened to her phone messages. There was one from Blake, asking her to have dinner with him. She looked over her shoulder, expecting to see David standing there with a pained expression.

Vera's voice echoed in her mind. *He said it would kill him all over again...*

She quickly punched the erase button.

Capone wandered into the kitchen and harassed her for his dinner. She opened a can of Kitty Bits and dumped it unceremoniously in his bowl. Capone looked at her as if to say, "What? No sprig of parsley on top?"

She searched the freezer for something for her own dinner, and emerged with the bean burrito. She was just desperate enough to eat it. How bad could it be?

She wrapped it in a paper towel and stuck it in the microwave. The moment she pushed the cook button, everything went dark.

Damn. The microwave had thrown a breaker.

She shuffled across the kitchen floor, careful not to get between Capone and his dinner, which he slurped noisily in the dark. Retrieving a flashlight from the table beside the door and steeling herself against childhood phobias, she opened the basement door and flipped the light switch for the return trip.

The musty scent of damp cardboard and mothballs assaulted her nostrils. She shone the beam of the flashlight down the stairs, looking for pairs of tiny eyes, or dangling spiders, or a swirling pit of demons.

Finding nothing except a little bit of dust and a lot of darkness, she made her way down the rickety stairs, holding on to the equally rickety handrail. Dodging stacks of boxes, she located the breaker box on a wall and shone the flashlight beam on it.

As she suspected, the switches for the entire kitchen side of the house had been thrown. She pushed them back into line with the rest of the switches in the box, and the basement light blazed to life.

"Reeooww."

She looked down. Capone sat at her feet, tangled in a string of Christmas lights. The kind David used to string on the shrubbery outside.

She untangled the cat and said, "There you go, buddy. Go find some mice."

She headed for the steps, Capone at her heels. When she looked down at him again, he was dragging the string of lights in his mouth. Astrid removed it, and scooped him into her arms. Or rather, shoveled his fat butt off the floor and onto her hip.

She struggled to the top of the stairs. "You really need to lose some weight."

She slammed the basement door. Capone scratched at it.

"What? You want to go back down there?"

"Reeooww."

"No. It's dirty." She went back over to the microwave and gave the burrito another shot, and the electricity went off again. And that's when she knew.

David wanted her to put up the outdoor lights.

December 17, 10:00 p.m.

EVENTUALLY, she gave up trying to argue with David.

He kept turning the electricity off until she finally turned it back on and hauled the strings of outdoor lights up from the basement.

And that's how Astrid Martin found herself out on the lawn at ten o'clock at night, in twenty-degree weather, wrapping the last string of Christmas bulbs around the slender branches of a Japanese maple.

It was the only way she was going to get to eat her crappy burrito.

Capone sat in the bow window of the living room, watching her.

"Are you enjoying yourself?" she yelled.

She could have sworn he was laughing at her.

CHAPTER 6

Saturday, December 22, 8:30 a.m.

Blake called several times over the next few days, and twice that Saturday morning. Astrid didn't answer the phone. She just couldn't. Every time she saw Blake's number on the caller ID, she'd think about her conversation with Vera.

God, she just wanted to get through this. She wanted to grieve in peace, let Christmas and New Year's slide by, and bury herself in work until the spring thaw.

Then maybe she'd take a vacation. Somewhere warm. Somewhere far away.

She stuffed her elf costume into a plastic grocery bag and headed for the mall. Three more days until Christmas. Two more shifts at the R.U.F.F. booth, and she'd have done her time. If she could only get through it without seeing Blake.

Unfortunately, that was not to be.

As soon as she arrived at the booth, he materialized at the end of the line.

"I see your friend is back," Edith said with a smile.

"I guess so."

"You don't seem too thrilled about it," Carla observed.

"Truthfully, I don't know what I'm feeling."

On the one hand, she wanted to blow him off. Tell him she wasn't ready for friendship, or anything else.

On the other hand, just seeing him made her feel better. Made her feel as if she had someone to weather the Christmas storm with. Someone who couldn't float, or walk through walls.

Being away from home somehow made David's presence seem less pressing. It made her want things she shouldn't want. Like friendships with handsome widowers.

Blake drew closer with every gift she wrapped, and by the time he stood before her, her stomach was in knots.

"Hello, Astrid."

"Hi, Blake."

"I've been calling you."

"You have? I've been really busy—"

"Astrid, don't." He put a box on the table for her to wrap. "I thought we had a nice time the other day. I got the impression you wouldn't mind if I called."

She tore a piece of wrapping paper off the giant roll. "I didn't think I would, either. But I guess I thought about it, and realized I'm not completely comfortable yet…"

"That's too bad. I was hoping you'd let me cook dinner for you. I have a great recipe."

And he cooks, too?

It was almost too much to bear.

Edith, who had been not-so-subtly listening in on the conversation, leaned over from her section of the table and said, "If Astrid isn't going to take you up on that offer, I will."

"What about Harvey?" Carla interjected.

"Oh, shut up," Edith said.

"Will you excuse us for a minute?" Astrid came around to the outside of the booth and took Blake by the elbow, dragging him to the only wooden bench nearby that wasn't occupied by a gaggle of senior citizens or a frazzled mother and her screaming kids.

"Listen, I'd love to come to dinner, but I'd feel a little bit guilty leaving my husband home alone—"

She stopped when she saw the look on Blake's face. The look that said, "Wow, is this woman a Froot Loop or what?"

She shook her head. "Wait. I mean, I'd feel like I was betraying him, somehow. It hasn't even been a year since his death."

Just 361 days, two hours and nine minutes.

Blake's features softened. "Astrid, I'm not trying to make you feel guilty. I just want to cook dinner for a friend. Will you let me?"

What was she doing here? By saying no to Blake, was she saying she didn't trust herself? Was she saying she couldn't keep things platonic between them? Couldn't have a friend?

"What are you making?"

He grinned. "Chicken curry with jasmine rice."

"I love chicken curry."

"So you'll come?"

She nodded. "I guess a girl has to eat, right?"

"Absolutely. How about tonight, around six-thirty? You bring the wine."

"Tonight?"

"I don't want to give you a chance to change your mind."

She hesitated. "Okay. Tonight at six-thirty."

Blake took a slip of paper out of his pocket and handed it to her. "Here's my address."

"Wow. You were pretty confident I'd say yes, huh?"

"Not confident. Hopeful."

He gave her a peck on the cheek and hurried off, the package she'd just wrapped tucked beneath his arm.

"Six-thirty," he called over his shoulder. "Don't be late. Chicken curry is terrible when it's dried out."

* * *

December 22, 6:28 p.m.

ASTRID PARKED in front of Blake's house and sat in her car, attempting to bolster her nerve by listening to a little Aretha Franklin. To say she was slightly nervous would be like saying the Pope was slightly Catholic.

She studied the house. It was a pleasant-looking refurbished Victorian in a neighborhood that had seen a recent resurgence in small-town charm. A few blocks away, a retro clothing store, an antique shop, a coffee house and a high-end Mexican restaurant had all taken up residence.

She could imagine Blake coming home here to his children and his wife. Raking leaves in the fall, washing the car in the driveway in the spring…

Before she could chicken out and leave, Blake stepped out onto the wide porch and waved to her.

Busted.

She turned off the car engine, took a deep breath, and grabbed the bottle of wine from the passenger seat.

"Hi," he said, as she made her way up the stone walkway to the house. "I was afraid you wouldn't show."

"Not me. I never miss a home-cooked meal." She handed him the bottle of wine.

He laughed, a low chuckle with just a hint of nerves, and held the door open for her. "Come in. Dinner's almost ready."

She stepped into a Victorian doll's house.

Colorful oriental carpets covered polished oak floors. The walls were stenciled in a lush flower pattern above white wainscoting, and a built-in bookcase held shelves of old books. A gray-and-white cat lay curled up on a wide windowsill overlooking the front porch.

A fire burned in the fireplace. A Christmas tree stood in the corner, surrounded by gifts and, yes, even an old-fashioned electric train track.

"Wow. Is this the North Pole?" she said.

"Thought I'd make you feel at home. Only you didn't wear the elf suit."

"It's at the cleaners'."

Blake excused himself to go open the wine while Astrid wandered over to the tree, examining the ornaments. Beautiful antique hand-blown glass, tin Victorian candle holders, tiny pictures in frames.

"Are these pictures of your family?"

Blake came back into the room and handed her a glass of wine. "Yes." He touched one of the pictures. "This is my oldest daughter, Tammy, and her husband, Ron. And this is their son, Robbie, and here's their daughter, Brenna."

He touched each picture as he said their names, making the ornaments spin lazily on the branches.

"Who is this?"

"That's my other daughter, Sheila, with her

husband, Paul, and here's their new son, Zack. He's ten months old. And this one is my youngest, my son, Jeff. He just got home from college a couple of days ago. He's out with some friends."

She touched another ornament. "Is this your wife?"

"Yes, that's Christine. It was taken a couple of Christmases before she was diagnosed."

A woman with chestnut hair and lively blue eyes gazed out from the picture, so full of life it was difficult to imagine her sick.

"She's beautiful. And she did a wonderful job with the house."

Blake's ears turned crimson. "Actually, this wasn't our home when Christine was alive. The kids and I moved here after she died. Too many memories at the other place."

"Oh, I'm sorry. I just assumed... I mean, the house looks..."

"Like it has a woman's touch?"

"Something like that."

Blake moved away from the tree and sat in a chair near the fireplace. "A designer helped me with the restoration. I felt like a Victorian home should have somewhat of a lighter feel. Besides, I had two daughters and I didn't want them to think that just because their mother was gone, they'd be forced to live in a completely masculine world."

"That was very thoughtful of you."

"Well, they helped me get through Christine's death as much as I helped them."

Astrid took a sip of her wine. "How long did it take you to finish everything?"

Blake laughed. "It's never really finished. I'm having the plumbing redone next month. It's in pretty bad shape." He stood. "Would you like a tour?"

"Sure. That would be great."

Blake showed her the rest of the house, for which he exhibited an obvious pride. Then he escorted her into the dining room, where the table was laid out in china and crystal.

"You didn't have to go to all this trouble," Astrid said.

"No trouble. I enjoy it." He pulled out her chair before disappearing into the kitchen. He returned with a platter of steaming chicken curry, vegetables and a bowl of fragrant jasmine rice.

"Smells wonderful," she said as he spooned food onto her plate. She tasted it. "Delicious."

"I took cooking classes after Christina died."

Astrid put her fork down. "I don't know how you did it. I can barely get through the day, and the only person I have to worry about is myself."

Blake gave her a sympathetic look. "Doing things, like the house and cooking, I guess it was my way of dealing with everything."

"I'm a counter, myself."

"A counter?"

"I count everything. Like how many loads of laundry I've done since David died. Eighty-four. And how many times I've swept the sidewalk. A hundred and forty. And how many cans of soup I've eaten. Fifty-seven."

"Fifty-seven cans of soup?" Blake refilled her wineglass. "Don't you cook?"

Astrid shook her head. "I can get by, but I'm lucky frozen foods and the miracle of microwave technology preceded me. Without them, I'd probably starve."

"That's too bad. Cooking can be very relaxing."

"So is sitting on the couch with a microwave dinner."

Blake laughed. "You're a very funny woman, Astrid."

"Funny strange, or funny ha-ha?"

He regarded her for a moment. "Both."

"I'll drink to that."

They touched wineglasses and looked at one another, startled by the mixture of anxiety and intrigue mirrored in each other's eyes.

The spell was broken by the sound of the front door slamming.

"In here, Jeff," Blake called.

A teenager who could have been Blake twenty-five years ago bobbed into the room. Same hazel eyes and chocolate-brown hair. Same easy smile.

"Hey."

"Hi," Blake said. "Did you have a good time?"

Jeff nodded, his glance sliding to Astrid.

"This is my friend, Astrid Martin."

"Oh, right. The wrapping elf. Nice to meet you." Jeff stretched a long arm across the table and shook Astrid's hand. His smile seemed genuine, even if he made it clear he was sizing her up.

"Nice to meet you, too."

With a jolt, Astrid realized that Blake had actually told his children about her. She wondered what, exactly, he'd said.

For a moment—no longer than the flicker of a candle—she let herself imagine what it would be like to be something more than friends with Blake. To be welcomed as part of his family. Accepted as one of them.

And then she blew that candle out.

No matter how nice it would be to be part of a big family at Christmas time, that wasn't her reality. Her reality was that she had her own family at home. She had Capone and David. And that was plenty.

Astrid rose. "I've got to get going."

Blake stood, too. "Really? Already?"

"I have some things to do. I don't want to interrupt you two. I'll leave you to whatever it is guys do."

"Oh, you know. Burp. Scratch. Exchange recipes." Jeff grinned.

"Yeah, and then we have a secret meeting of the He-Man Woman-Haters' Club."

"Gee, I'm sorry I'm going to miss that."

Blake followed her to the front door.

"Thanks for everything," Astrid said as Blake helped her on with her coat. "Dinner was wonderful."

"I'm glad you could make it."

"Me, too."

"So, you want to do something tomorrow?"

"Tomorrow?"

"I'm sorry. I don't mean to push. It's just nice to be with someone who understands how difficult this time of year can be."

"I know."

But even as she said it, Astrid realized the holidays weren't turning out to be quite as difficult as she'd thought they would be.

And she wasn't really sure if that was a good thing.

CHAPTER 7

Sunday, December 23, 5:30 p.m.

Despite her earlier trepidation, Astrid had woken up in a good mood, and agreed to meet Blake for breakfast. Afterward, they'd gone hunting for Victorian doorknobs at a few local antique shops.

For lunch they discovered a wonderful little café that served panini and authentic Italian gelato, and while they slurped the heavenly concoction, Blake had asked her to join him for a holiday fund-raiser to benefit the refurbished art deco movie theater on Main Street.

There would be a silent auction in the lobby, and then they'd show *North by Northwest*, one of Astrid's all-time favorite movies, on the big screen.

When Blake had dropped Astrid off at home that afternoon, he'd walked her to her doorstep, no doubt expecting to be invited in. She'd politely closed the door in his face.

She felt terrible about it, but she just couldn't

have him there with David. It would just be too weird.

She knew she couldn't avoid inviting Blake into her home forever, but she was hoping she could put it off at least until after the holidays. His daughters and their husbands and children were due in the next day, so she probably wouldn't even see Blake until after New Year's.

In the meantime, she would explain things to David so he wouldn't get the wrong idea.

Assuming ghosts actually *got* ideas.

Astrid rooted through her closet, choosing and discarding half a dozen dresses. Her floor looked like the changing room at a department store after a one-day sale.

She couldn't figure out why she was so nervous. It was just Blake.

Capone ambled in, his purr as melodic as a lawn-mower and almost as loud. He tiptoed gingerly over the fifty-dollar cocktail dress she'd picked up at a discount store and curled up on the two-hundred-and-fifty-dollar number. The cat had taste.

"Hey. I was going to wear that," she said.

Capone rolled onto his back and closed his eyes.

"You're right. It's probably too much."

She fished a simple, knee-length black skirt and a red satin blouse out of the closet. Perfect.

She was just putting her jewelry on when the

doorbell rang. Astrid took a deep breath. "Okay, Capone, how do I look?"

Capone half opened his eyes, yawned, and went back to sleep.

"Thanks. That's really flattering."

At the last minute, she pulled the love-knot ring from her finger and set it on her dresser. It didn't really go with what she was wearing.

No, the truth was, it didn't really go with what she was *feeling*.

"No offense, David. But I want to go this one alone."

Capone opened his eyes and gave her a knowing look.

"Go back to sleep," she said.

Then she slipped into her shoes and coat and met Blake on the front steps, locking the door behind her.

December 23, 11:30 p.m.

SNOWFLAKES had begun to fall steadily by the time Astrid and Blake made it back to her place. He escorted her up the walk, holding her elbow so she wouldn't slip on the slick stones.

The cold flakes melted on her cheeks and eyelashes. She caught one on her tongue and laughed. Blake hugged her to him. The scent of his cologne, mixed with the frosty damp of new snow, enveloped her. Astrid held her breath, and not because of the cologne.

He was going to kiss her. Heaven help her, he was going to *kiss* her!

She wanted to stop him...

No, that was a lie. She wanted to *want* to stop him, but she didn't.

She wanted to *want* to think of David, and how she shouldn't be waiting for a kiss from another man just three hundred and sixty-two days after he died.

But she didn't.

She closed her eyes. The touch of Blake's lips on hers was as soft as a snowflake, but warm. So incredibly warm. He slid his arms around her waist, pulling her closer, deepening the kiss.

It was a kiss like the ones they write about in romance novels, starting off sweet and then building, until it was filled with heat and hunger and desire. It was the kind of kiss they sang about in songs, melancholy and hopeful all at once.

It was the kind of kiss that could easily lead to tangled sheets and midnight omelets.

Astrid melted in Blake's arms, sliding her hands beneath his suit coat and warming them against his sides. His ribcage rose and fell against her palms with each breath, the warmth and movement a testament to life.

Blake was a living, breathing man. Tangible proof that life went on, even when husbands sometimes didn't.

How in the world could David's ghost ever compete with that?

Astrid pulled away and looked up at Blake. The porch light behind him reflected a halo of falling snow. He looked like an angel. A savior.

But was she really ready to be saved?

She escaped his embrace. "I have to go."

"Astrid, spend Christmas Eve with me. With my family—"

She reached up and touched his lips with her forefinger and shook her head. "I can't. I need to be alone."

She unlocked her front door and slipped inside, leaving Blake standing beneath the porch light, snowflakes catching in his dark hair, turning it to white.

Astrid leaned against the inside of the door and closed her eyes. "Forgive me," she whispered.

Only, she didn't know if she was talking to David or Blake.

Monday, December 24, 8:45 a.m.

ASTRID ARRIVED at work to discover that Vera Tait had passed away the day before. There was to be a memorial service for her on Thursday.

Since she had no family, Vera had requested that Astrid take care of her personal effects.

Astrid sorted through a drawer filled with pictures

from the Taits' travels. London, Munich, Rome, Paris, Madrid. She could have been looking at her own photo albums.

She found one in which Vera and Milton stood on the Great Wall of China, and set it aside. She would have it enlarged for Vera's memorial service. She also found the necklace, the one Milton had given Vera for their first anniversary—the one Vera had credited with her ability to hear Milton—and put it in an envelope to be sent to the funeral home. Vera had requested to be buried wearing it.

When she was finished, Astrid had divided Vera's belongings into three piles. One for items to be donated to local charity organizations, one for items to be sent to Vera's cousin in Minnesota and one for stuff to be thrown away.

Astrid sat in the recliner and stared out at the terrible view, thinking how sad it was that Vera Tait's life had been reduced to this. Three piles.

No one to mourn her. No one to miss her. Just three piles.

Is that how her own life would end?

She tucked the necklace and the picture of the Taits in her pocket, turned off the light and closed the door.

December 24, 6:30 p.m.

ASTRID SWITCHED OFF the television, unable to find anything that wasn't Christmas-related except for a

Korean soap opera and a jewelry marathon on the Home Shopping Network.

Capone pawed the tassels on her afghan, giving her a look.

"No, we're not watching *Miracle on 34th Street.* I'm not in the mood."

"Reeoww."

"No!"

She twisted the love-knot ring on her finger, trying to recall what she and David had been doing at that exact moment last year. Eating dinner, just the two of them, and looking forward to a night in front of the fire with a good bottle of wine.

Before she knew it, Astrid's thoughts had strayed to Blake and his family, who were no doubt gathered around the dining-room table, laughing and talking and exchanging gifts as they shared a wonderful meal.

Or maybe they were cuddled up on the giant couch, eating popcorn, watching *It's a Wonderful Life.*

Just thinking about it made her ache for company.

Perhaps if David understood her reasons. Perhaps if he knew how lonely she was, he would tell her to go.

Astrid lit the candles on the end table and turned off all the lights except those on the Christmas tree. She wound up the music box on the mantel and sat back down on the couch, closing her eyes. She touched her ring.

"David, where are you?"

She held her breath, but felt nothing.

David David David David…

She opened her eyes. The house felt chilly. Empty. It held none of the warmth she'd sensed over the past few weeks, when David had been telling her what to do. When he'd been there beside her, helping her get through the worst of things.

Was it any coincidence that now, when she needed him the most, he wasn't there? That after she'd done everything he'd asked of her and now wanted something from him, he was nowhere to be felt?

She blew out the candles and turned on the lights.

Maybe it was unfair of her to search for him when all she wanted was permission to spend time with another man. Unfair to ask David to let her go. Or maybe…

Maybe he'd never been there at all.

Astrid suddenly felt very alone.

She looked at the tree, and the decorations, and the cookies piled high on a tray on the coffee table as if someone were stopping by.

It was ridiculous.

No, it was worse than ridiculous. It was sad.

She'd wanted David back so badly that she gave up something real to be with his ghost. A real friend. Someone who could have truly comforted her that night.

What a fool she was.

Capone jumped up on her lap and pushed his head beneath her chin. His purring eased the painful lump that had formed in her throat.

Maybe she was being too hard on herself. Maybe she'd just needed something to hold on to, and had grasped at any little thing that reminded her of David. All those little coincidental events that led her to believe he wasn't quite gone.

But she didn't need those things, really. She would always have her memories of David. Nothing could erase them. Not 363 days. Not 3,063 days.

Tears burned behind her eyes as she buried her face in Capone's neck.

"Oh, David. I miss you so much."

The phone rang, startling her. She wiped her eyes on her sleeve before picking it up.

"Astrid, it's Blake."

"Oh, hello. Merry Christmas."

"Merry Christmas. Listen, I hate to bother you, but I have a problem."

"What is it? What's going on?"

"A pipe burst in the kitchen, and the place is a mess. The dining room is flooded. The lights on the tree shorted out. And the thing is, I hate to disappoint the kids—"

"Bring them here. Bring everyone."

"Really?"

"Really."

"I know you wanted to be alone…"

"Bring them."

Blake was quiet for a moment, and then he said, "Thank you, Astrid. We'll see you soon."

She could hear the relief in his voice—and the hopefulness, too.

She didn't know what she wanted from him, besides friendship and comfort. But she supposed she'd work it out, one day at a time.

Astrid nudged Capone from her lap. "Get moving, buddy. We're having company for Christmas."

CHAPTER 8

December 24, 8:30 p.m.

Astrid carried a tray laden with mugs of hot chocolate and Christmas cookies into the living room.

Blake and his family had come bearing the full Christmas Eve feast they'd planned to serve at Blake's house, and now they were all too full to move.

But never, they agreed, never too full for Christmas cookies.

On the television, George Bailey was trying to figure out the meaning of life. But in Astrid's living room, for Blake and his children and grandchildren, there was little question about that.

Astrid was a little envious, but mostly grateful, that she was able to share in it, even if she was just hovering around the edges.

"Okay, everybody. Let's do presents," Blake said. He dragged two big green plastic bags out of the corner and dumped a pile of gifts in the middle of the living-room floor.

The children shrieked and giggled as he handed them gift after gift.

Tammy was the recipient of the beautiful silk scarf Astrid had wrapped the first time she'd met Blake at the mall. Sheila received the glass bowl.

And then, to her surprise, Blake handed *her* a gift.

"What's this?" She recognized her own handiwork in the wrapping. But she had no idea what was in the box.

"When I saw it, I knew I had to get it for you," Blake said.

Astrid was confused. "But you hardly knew me when I wrapped this gift for you."

She peeled the paper off and opened the box, folding back the tissue paper inside to reveal a teapot painted with irises and ivy.

She felt the blood drain from her cheeks.

"What? Astrid, what is it?"

She grabbed Blake's hand and pulled him into the dining room, opening the china cabinet. Inside were eight cups and eight saucers in the exact same pattern.

"I broke the teapot a couple of years ago," she said.

Blake didn't look the least bit surprised.

"What's going on?" she whispered. "How could you possibly have known?"

Blake shook his head. "You're going to think I'm crazy."

"Tell me," she pleaded.

He blew out a breath. "I don't know. A few weeks ago I started hearing this voice." He shook his head. "No, I didn't hear it, exactly. But it was like something, someone, was compelling me to do certain things."

Astrid's breathing grew shallow. "Go on."

Blake shrugged. "I got this, this *message* to go to the wrapping booth. To talk to you and ask you to coffee. It was like a compulsion. Just like buying this teapot."

Astrid's knees felt weak.

"I don't understand it, Astrid. But after I met you, I decided I wouldn't question it. I'm so glad to know you, no matter the circumstances."

Astrid leaned against the china cabinet, clutching the teapot to her chest.

Blake touched her elbow. "Are you okay?"

"I just need a minute."

"Of course." He kissed her forehead lightly. "I'll meet you back in the living room."

Astrid's hands shook as she slid the teapot into place amongst the teacups and saucers.

How? *How?*

She returned to the living room and joined Blake on the couch. They watched Blake's grandchildren play with their new toys, the lights of the Christmas tree glowing behind them, and the sound of the music box playing on the fireplace mantel.

And that's when Astrid knew, with no uncertainty, that David had planned it all. He'd given her one final Christmas gift—perhaps the best one ever.

He'd given her permission to stop counting the days she'd lived without him, and start counting the days she was lucky to be alive.

Capone jumped up and settled in her lap, his tail tickling her nose.

"Merry Christmas, Astrid," Blake said in a low voice.

"Merry Christmas," she said.

* * * * *

SECRET SANTA

LISA CHILDS

From the Author

Dear Reader,

Happy holidays!

I'm thrilled to be part of the Harlequin NEXT Christmas anthology. I love the holiday season, but I'm definitely one of those people who takes way too much upon herself to make the holidays special for everyone else. I cook huge family dinners and bake cookies and make fudge to give away as special presents. I go broke trying to get everything my daughters put on their Christmas lists. My feet ache from shopping for everyone, and I take very little time for myself.

So I identify very much with Maggie O'Brien, and I love that the most special of all the gifts Maggie receives this Christmas is time for herself.

With the holidays fast approaching, I'm going to try to carve out some time for myself, but to me, it's not Christmas unless it's crazy. So I'll see you in the malls—I'll be the one with cookie dough in her hair and a smile on her face. This year I hope Santa brings you everything on your list!

Lisa Childs

To Tara Gavin. I can't thank you enough for everything!
Happy holidays!

For my daughters, Ashley and Chloe, who don't believe
in Santa Claus anymore but who have always believed
in their mother!

For my husband, Paul, my ever-supportive
and loving not-so-secret Santa!

CHAPTER 1

"Silent Night…"

Maggie O'Brien's breath escaped her aching lungs in little puffs of white mist. Her fingers numb, she struggled to turn the key in the ignition. A nail chipped against the metal, the snap of the cuticle the only sound in the interior of her minivan. Not a gear ground or a crank spun, the engine refused to start, the battery completely dead.

Maggie slumped forward and rested her forehead against the steering wheel, the plastic cold and hard against her skin. "Damn, damn, damn…"

If only she hadn't turned off the van…

But after the grocery store, she'd stopped back at the office to drop off the coffee and filters she'd bought, just in case someone beat her to work in the morning and wanted to brew a pot. But in the seven years she'd been employed at the insurance agency no one had *ever* beaten her to work and no one made coffee but her.

A sigh slipped through her lips, forming another wispy white cloud that floated toward the frosted windshield. She uncurled one cold hand from the wheel and reached to the passenger's seat, fumbling in her open purse for her cell phone. At least she only had to maneuver her stiff fingers to push one button to speed dial the garage that regularly serviced her lemon. While the phone rang, she glanced at her watch; the illuminated dial read seven. Fortunately the garage had twenty-four-hour tow service. She waited for the click of the call-forward, but someone answered, "Mallehan."

Her heart kicked against her ribs at the low rasp of the male voice. "Hi...you're still there?"

"Maggie?"

Her heart rate quickened, spreading warmth through her despite the bite of the December night. "I call so often you recognize my voice?" She'd like to think that was why she recognized his, but he usually didn't answer his phone. He had a secretary.

Patrick Mallehan chuckled. "If you ever replace that heap, I'm going to start missing mortgage payments, Maggie."

"Glad I'm putting a roof over your head." Since her divorce six years ago, she'd struggled to keep a roof over her own and her kids' heads. Now with one in college, one playing high-school hockey and another with a video-game addiction, the providing-shelter thing had gotten even trickier and was why she hadn't replaced the lemon with a new car.

He chuckled again, then asked, "Where are you?"

"At the office." Where she spent entirely too much of her time.

"That's good—"

"Breaking down is never good—"

"But at least you're warm," he said, his deep voice so full of warmth her ear tingled.

But maybe the tingling had nothing to do with his voice and everything to do with frostbite.

"It's freezing out there tonight," he added.

"Yes, it is." She should have gone back in the office to call; that would have made sense. "The van's completely dead. How soon can a truck get here?"

She glanced again at her watch. While she was grocery shopping, the kids had called to let her know they were heading to the mall to catch a movie. She doubted they'd be home yet, so she would need a ride. "Do you think the driver can drop me home?" He had before.

"Sure, Maggie. It'll be just a few minutes," he assured her. "Sit tight."

He broke the connection, leaving Maggie feeling bereft. Without the warmth of Patrick Mallehan's voice, she shivered with cold, her teeth clicking together. She peered through the frosted window toward the office, which occupied a corner of a small strip mall. They shared the space with a dog groomer, a beauty parlor and a tobacco store. Because her boss was cheap, they turned down the heat after hours. With lots of windows and thin walls, the office wouldn't be much warmer than the van.

He had said just a few minutes, and Patrick Mallehan was always true to his word. That was why his service stations—he had four locations—were so successful. He was that rare mechanic that a customer could trust. Before she could have unlocked the office door, had she decided to wait inside, a Mallehan tow truck, black with a light bar on the roof, pulled into the parking lot.

She breathed a sigh of relief, filling the van with white mist. As she opened her door and stepped out, the driver hopped down from the tow truck, landing on the pavement right in front of her: six feet plus of Patrick Mallehan, proprietor of Mallehan Service Stations.

"It's…you," she murmured, surprised that he'd personally make a service call.

He chuckled. "Hey, I may be a little out of practice, but I remember how to hook up a tow."

Maggie was a little out of practice, too, with how to react to a man like him. She resisted the urge to check her hair and makeup in the side mirror. Was her red hair a mess, standing on end? Had her eyeliner run so that it rimmed her green eyes? Maybe it was better that she didn't know.

She tipped back her head, so she could meet his gaze, his blue eyes gleaming in the glow of the parking-lot lights. Damn, he was tall and broad, his shoulders testing the seams of his black leather jacket. A navy-blue sweater stretched across his chest and dark jeans hugged his lean hips and long legs.

"Damn, it's cold," Mallehan said, his big hands closing over hers. "Where are your gloves?"

"My daughter borrowed them." Because Kirsten couldn't remember where she'd left hers—at home or in the college dorm.

He wore no gloves, but his skin was warm, chasing the chill from her fingers, which tingled now as feeling, probably too much feeling, rushed back. As Kirsten would have said, the man was *hot*. Embarrassment heated her face. Kirsten could call guys hot; she was twenty. Maggie was not.

"Why didn't you wait inside?" he asked.

She cleared her throat, refusing to act like a tongue-tied adolescent. "You know how cheap Hal is. There's as much frost on the office windows as the van's."

"The wrecker is nice and warm," he said, tugging her toward the passenger's side of the big tow truck. He released her hands, then opened the door.

A wave of warm air and Christmas music enveloped Maggie. If not for the lure of the heat blowing full blast from the vents, Maggie would have stepped back. But she only shuddered over the carols drifting from the truck radio.

"You're shivering," Patrick Mallehan said. "Hop up."

Maggie eyed the distance between the asphalt—looking as if salted with the small, hard pebbles of snow—and the shiny running board of the truck. God, she'd probably rip the seam on her favorite dress pants, the slimming black ones with the thin blue pinstripes, if she tried to stretch a leg up that high.

Big hands gripped her waist, lifting her off the ground. Maggie's heart lurched, and she covered his hands with hers, holding on as he raised her toward the running board.

"Careful," he said, "don't hit your head."

She wasn't worried about her head; the erratic beat of her heart elicited more concern. But she ducked anyway. As her butt settled onto the seat, Patrick squeezed her knee. "Warm up. There's coffee in the holder. I didn't touch it yet. Help yourself."

Before she could thank him, he shut the door, closing her in with the Christmas music—James Brown-style.

At least it wasn't traditional. The truck cab was warm, and she had coffee. She reached for the paper cup, closing her thawing fingers around the cardboard protective sleeve. If she had caffeine after noon, she couldn't get more than a couple of hours' sleep. She clutched the cup tightly, savoring its warmth. Then she dipped her head near the plastic cover, breathing in the rich scent of coffee, chocolate and peppermint. Hunger tightened the muscles of her stomach, prodding her to take a sip.

"Just a sip," she murmured. One sip wouldn't keep her awake. As Patrick vaulted into the truck and folded his long, lean body into the driver's seat, she acknowledged it probably wouldn't be the caffeine keeping her awake but thoughts of Patrick Mallehan…dreams of him.

God, she might need to check her license to remind herself she wasn't twenty and at the mercy of hormones all the time, just once a month.

"You can have the whole cup," Patrick said, as he shifted the truck, backing the winch to the front of her van.

"What?"

"The coffee. You don't have to just sip. It's all yours."

She slurped, swallowing a warm, sweet mouthful. "Mmm…" She licked her lips, then glanced up to find his gaze focused on her mouth. "Mustache?"

He shook his head. "No, you got it."

So she *had* had a mustache. At least she'd

removed it more easily than a wax treatment. "I never would have figured you for the peppermint-mocha type," she said.

He chuckled. "Oh, I have quite an appetite for sweets."

"A sweet tooth."

"Something like that," he murmured as he put the truck in park and hopped down from the cab. The grinding of the winch as he hooked up her van mercifully drowned out the Christmas music.

Maggie was a Scrooge by necessity rather than nature. Since she'd become a single mother, she couldn't deal with the commercialism of Christmas…because she couldn't afford it. Another auto-repair bill would deflate her Christmas funds even more. The kids didn't understand that their Christmas lists were less important than shelter, transportation and food.

Her stomach rumbled, reminding her that she hadn't had any food since lunch. Cradling the cup in both hands, she slurped down another mouthful of the sweet peppermint mocha.

The driver's door flew open again, and Patrick got back into the truck. "Let's hope I remembered how to hook up."

"I won't be upset if we lose the van," Maggie admitted. She'd thought about pulling a Seinfeld and leaving the keys in her vehicle in a bad area of town. But the lemon probably wouldn't start for anyone to steal it.

Patrick chuckled. "Since we already replaced the battery, it has to be the alternator this time."

"I'll take your word for it," she said.

"Not many people trust mechanics," he said, his jaw tensing. "When something breaks on a car I just fixed, I usually get accused of rigging the breakdown so I can charge for another repair."

"Those must be people who don't know you," she assured him, "or they're crazy." They got a lot of crazies at the insurance office, usually at five minutes before closing.

He chuckled and said, "Oh, Maggie, this is why I hope you never buy a new car. I'd miss you."

"Well, since we both know how cheap Hal is, you can bet I'm not going to be able to afford a new car for a while," she said. Not unless she got a bigger raise than the measly annual increase Hal gave. "But once you replace every part of the engine, I won't need one."

"True."

The last thing she needed during the holiday season was another unplanned expense. No, the last thing she needed was to lose her transportation. "You probably almost already have."

"Almost," he agreed. "If it's just the alternator, I'll have it back to you tomorrow."

She breathed a sigh of relief. "Thanks."

"Hey, I have to keep my favorite customer happy."

"Your most frequent customer," she said.

He turned his head toward her, his eyes twinkling in the dashboard lights. "Even if I didn't see you so often, Maggie, you'd still be my favorite."

No matter the age on her driver's license, this man tongue-tied her. Heat flushed her face. Instead of stammering out what probably even her ten-year-old would have labeled a lame comeback, she pressed her mouth against the plastic lid of the coffee and took another deep swallow. When she lowered the paper cup, her porch light glinted through the windshield and sparkled against the black hood of the tow truck. "This is my house," she observed. "You know where I live?"

"Your address is always on the invoice, Maggie," Patrick reminded her. "So yeah, I know where you live."

Her face burned with another wave of embarrassment. Of course he'd know her address; he'd sent more than one invoice to her. He wasn't twenty either, with hormones prompting him to find her house and drive past again and again, hoping to catch a glimpse of her. Had any man ever done that for her? Her ex-husband hadn't; he'd never made much of an effort to impress her.

"Thanks for dropping me off," she said.

"Do you need a ride in the morning, to work?" he asked. "I can pick you up."

He could, if he was interested. But Maggie didn't have time for another man in her life. Not right now. "No, that's all right. My daughter's home from college. I'll use her car or have her drop me off."

"If you're sure…"

"You don't need to go out of your way," she said.

"I'm just around the corner from you," he said. "Over in White Pine Ridge."

Of course. The private community of high-end homes. "That's a little more than around the corner."

"Well, I'm close, Maggie." And as he turned toward her in the cab of the big truck, he was *too* close.

She fumbled for the door handle. "Well, I'd better get in the house." Then she remembered her trip to the store after work. "Oh, I have groceries in the back of the van."

"Unlock your door, and I'll bring in your bags."

Which meant he'd be coming into her home. She had no idea in what condition the kids had left the house. She doubted it was tidy. They'd never quite learned to pick up after themselves. They took after their father more than they did her.

As she jumped down from the truck, the words of another new Christmas song chased her. She recognized the voice of Jon Bon Jovi as he sang, "Backdoor Santa…"

Minutes later Patrick Mallehan walked through her back door, his arms laden with bags of groceries. Under the fluorescent kitchen light, his hair gleamed golden, any white hidden beneath a dusting of snowflakes. Maggie reached up and ran her fingers through his hair, the strands soft and silky to her touch.

"It wasn't snowing that bad," she mused, as she brushed away the last of the flakes. He had only a stray white strand or two, nothing like the grays she hid beneath a cinnamon-red dye. If not for the fine lines rimming his deep-blue eyes, he might pass for twenty, but she knew he was forty-five because she'd checked the policies he'd taken out with her boss, his friend, the insurance agent.

He chuckled. "I knocked the snow off the back door of the van."

She shivered in commiseration, having dumped some snow on her head and down the nape of her neck because of that door. "That's another reason I should get rid of the van," she said. Realizing she was still touching him, she drew her hands back, then reached for the bags in his arms.

But he held tight to the handles, the plastic entwined around his big fingers. For a mechanic, he had amazingly clean hands, not a grease stain anywhere on his skin or under his clipped-short nails. "I'll set 'em down," he offered. "Just show me where."

Irritation frayed Maggie's nerves as she turned toward her cluttered counters. The children hadn't cleared away their dishes. Glasses with an inch of milk in the bottoms and plates thick with ketchup and crumbs covered every inch of the butcher block.

"Kids," she muttered, then pointed toward the oak trestle table in the corner of the country kitchen with the golden oak cupboards and butcher-block countertops. Oak wainscoting covered two-thirds of the walls; sunny yellow paint the upper third. "The table is good. You didn't have to bring these in for me. I've taken up enough of your night already. I can't imagine why you're working so late."

"Paperwork," he said, his handsome face twisting into a grimace.

"So coming to my rescue was just an excuse to get away from the books?" she teased as she started picking through the bags he'd dropped on the table.

"Do I need an excuse to see you, Maggie?"

Her heart lurched at his playful tone. Damn, the man was a flirt, and it had been so long since a man had flirted with Maggie that she'd forgotten how to react and how to flirt back. "Just a bad alternator," she said.

"Here's another bag," he said, drawing a small gift bag from inside his coat. "I almost missed it, it was tucked up under the third-row seat."

"That's not mine," she said. "I haven't even

started my Christmas shopping yet." Just the groceries so that she could bake the Christmas cookies and
fudge that she gave out to the newspaper boy and the
mailman and a few special customers at the insurance office. She'd considered baking some treats for
Patrick Mallehan, too, but she hadn't thought he
would appreciate the gift until tonight, until she'd
learned he had a sweet tooth.

"I didn't think *you* bought it. It says For Maggie
on the tag," he said, holding the metallic red bag
toward her.

The only presents she received since the divorce,
and even in the last few years before, were from the
kids, usually homemade gifts, on her birthday,
Mother's Day and Christmas. But not even Kirsten,
the college sophomore, dared to call her Maggie.
She was always Mom. Sometimes she felt as though
she were *only* Mom.

"It can't be for me," she insisted, shaking her head
as she stared at the bag.

"It has *your* name on it," Patrick pointed out. "It
was in *your* van."

She often left the doors unlocked, perhaps subcon-
sciously hoping for someone to steal the lemon…if
it happened to start for the thief. Really she left the
van unlocked because her kids always left things
inside and had to run out to retrieve MP3 players
or homework assignments or athletic equipment.

The small red package was none of those things. It was *hers*.

Her fingers trembling slightly, she reached for the metallic bag. She'd been so cold at the store that she'd tossed the grocery bags inside the van without ever noticing the package beneath the seat. "I can't imagine…it must be some mistake…"

"You're one of those, huh?" he mused cryptically.

The bag forgotten, she studied his face, trying to read the meaning of his little grin. "One of *those?*"

"The kind of woman who gives to everyone else but has trouble accepting anything for herself. A compliment. A gift."

For a mechanic, for a *man*, he was surprisingly insightful, uncomfortably insightful. He didn't know just engines; he understood people, too. He understood her.

Maggie shook off the fanciful thought. He couldn't understand her; he didn't even know her. He only knew her van and that it probably needed a new alternator. And that it had had this small gift shoved under the third-row seat.

"Thank you for picking up the van, Patrick, and for dropping me off," she said.

"You're trying to get rid of me," he said, chuckling. "You're not even going to let me see what you got in that little bag?"

She narrowed her eyes, then studied his handsome face, which was creased with a playful grin. "You peeked," she accused.

He shrugged, his broad shoulders moving easily beneath the supple leather of his expensive jacket. He must have been doing books tonight; he definitely hadn't been working on engines. His grin widening, he backed toward the door. "Now that you mention the time, it is getting late…"

"I hadn't mentioned the time," she said, following him across the linoleum toward the back door, as if she could intimidate a man who was at least a foot taller than she was. "You peeked!"

"I'll see you tomorrow," he promised as he opened the door only wide enough to squeeze through then quickly shut it behind himself.

Maggie thought about following him. But as a mom, she was used to having no privacy, and she really couldn't lecture him about peeking, not after he'd rescued her from freezing to death in the office parking lot. She stepped close to the kitchen window, intending to watch the lights of the tow truck as it pulled away from her house, but curiosity overwhelmed her and she opened the bag.

She counted three bottle caps, then pulled them out one at a time. First she found bath salts, Pure Seduction from Victoria's Secret. The second bottle was body wash, the third Love Spell lotion, each smelling better than the last.

Who would have gone to Victoria's Secret for her? The gift had to be a joke. Yet she was reluctant to put down the bag. But the groceries wouldn't put themselves away. She set the metallic red bag on the table and picked up the carton of eggs. Rarely did the whole dozen survive the trip home from the store in the van, so she flipped open the lid to check for cracks. She found them, but instead of oozing white or yellow yolk, the cracks had frozen. The *eggs* had frozen.

She set the carton back on the table. She wouldn't be baking tonight. As she reached for a gallon of milk, her nails scraped through frost on the plastic bottle. Patrick really had rescued her tonight. A smile pulled at her lips, but when she opened the refrigerator door to put the milk inside, her smile slid away. The kids' Christmas lists, held by magnets to the front of the fridge, fluttered in the breeze. All those things, all those expensive things…at least on Kirsten's and Cody's list. Brandon only wanted Santa—even at ten he still believed—to bring him one thing, but that was probably as expensive as everything combined on the other kids' lists, if she could even find the game system of which only limited supplies were available.

She had no idea how much an alternator would wind up costing her. But even if she didn't have yet another expense for the van, she couldn't afford to buy her children all the things they wanted.

While Maggie had been growing up, her mother had excelled at making her feel guilty. All Maggie made her kids feel was disappointment…especially Christmas morning. She sighed and picked up the metallic bag again, then headed toward her bathroom. A short while later she sank chin-deep into sweetly scented bubbles.

She'd stopped feeling guilty a long time ago, even before her mother had died. Maggie did the best she could for her kids. Maybe it was time she did something for herself. Maybe it was time she made her own Christmas list. While the bottles were nice, she didn't need anything material. She only needed time. Time for herself. She sighed and settled back into the warm, scented bubbles.

Then she closed her eyes and an image formed in her mind, a tall, golden-haired image of a grinning, teasing, flirting man. Patrick Mallehan…

She squeezed the shower gel into her hand and rubbed it over her bare shoulder. But she imagined his hand instead, big and broad, caressing her naked skin. Despite his flirting, she had as much chance of getting Patrick Mallehan as Brandon had of getting the game system he wanted.

She sighed, but a sudden cacophony outside the bathroom swallowed the sound of her breath. "I'm telling Mom how fast you drove," Brandon threatened his sister.

"You're still a tattletale. When are you ever going to grow up?" Kirsten griped.

"What the hell—" Cody bit off his expletive. "Mom! What's wrong with these eggs? They're sweating!"

Maggie grabbed up her bottles to put back in the metallic bag, but before she dropped them inside, she noticed a little envelope at the bottom. She dried her hands on the towel beside the tub then reached for the white envelope. The steam had unsealed the flap so the card slipped easily out into her hand.

"Maggie, treat yourself…like a woman…"

She shivered despite the warmth of the small, steamy bathroom. Who would have left her such a message? Who could be her *secret Santa*?

CHAPTER 2

"Deck the Halls…"

"Maggie, stop acting like such a Scrooge. You know you love Christmas," said the ex who'd never really known anything about the woman to whom he'd been married for fifteen years.

But then, to be fair, and Maggie was always fair, she hadn't known who she was either when they'd gotten married; she hadn't really known who she was until after their divorce. But if she'd known who *he* was twenty-one years ago, she never would have married him. Not that Derek was a bad man. He just wasn't much of a man. He was helpless. And to a woman who prized her independence above everything else, helplessness was almost as great an offense as infidelity.

"Maybe I *would* love Christmas," she admitted as she leaned back in her desk chair, "if I could afford it."

"Here we go again," Derek said with a heavy sigh

as if she always nagged him for money even though she rarely brought it up. "The Friend of the Court takes your child support out of my check every week and leaves me barely enough to afford my condo payment."

"And your car payment." *He* had a new car. "You can also afford to eat out." The Friend of the Court played favorites, definitely preferring Derek to Maggie.

Derek laughed. "I have to eat out. I don't know how to cook."

"You could learn."

"You could invite me over more often," he said, lowering his voice as he lowered his stocky body onto the corner of her desk.

She had an office, of sorts: two dark-paneled walls and a gray fabric room divider that separated without isolating her from the reception area. She'd brightened the gray divider with pictures of the kids and the pets who'd come and gone in their lives. And on her desk, the mammoth gray metal L-shaped unit always held a vase of flowers. Of course they were plastic; nothing living survived the flux in temperatures due to how low thrifty Hal programmed the thermostat for after hours.

"I love…your cooking, Maggie." Derek closed one big, brown eye in a wink, then grinned his boyish, dimple-piercing grin. Even at forty-four, he was more boy than man.

Maggie's traitorous pulse quickened for a moment, and she remembered why she'd married Derek. When she'd met him at twenty, she'd listened to her hormones instead of her heart, or maybe she'd gotten them mixed up. She and Derek had had a lot of chemistry in the beginning and occasionally after…even after their divorce. A couple of times when Derek had been without a girlfriend they'd gotten together. Just for a night or two. Just for sex. But Maggie had worried that the kids, Brandon especially, might pick up on the relationship and build hope that their parents were reuniting. That wasn't going to happen. She had three kids; she didn't want another.

"You're not seeing anyone?" she asked, wondering if her ex was her secret Santa. Did he want her to remember she was a woman now, when he needed a woman? But Derek never wanted just a woman; he wanted a mother.

"No, Marcia and I stopped seeing each other." He sighed his woeful, feel-sorry-for-me sigh. "She was too busy for me."

Too busy to wait on him hand and foot? Too busy to tend to his every whim and give him all her attention? Maggie understood being too busy; she'd been too busy for Derek for a long time, even before she'd finally asked for a divorce. "I'm sorry, Derek. Marcia was really nice." And smart. "The kids liked her."

He nodded, his brown eyes as pitiful as a kicked puppy's. "If we'd stayed together, she could have helped me buy the kids' gifts. But since she's not…"

"Derek, I told you—" not that he ever listened to her "—I don't even know when I'll get my van back so that I can do my own shopping."

"But you have to do your shopping anyway," he persisted, always the salesman. "You can do mine, too."

If he wouldn't shop for his kids, he wouldn't have gone shopping for her. He couldn't be her secret Santa. Her heart lifted, buoyant with relief. She didn't want a man, any man, who only wanted to be with her because he was scared of being alone.

"You can do this," she assured him. "They've made their lists."

"But I won't know which things you already bought them."

"That's easy. Nothing yet." And she didn't know when she'd have time to shop. Patrick had said the van would be done today; she reminded herself of that every time she picked up the phone to call him. To check on the van. Not just to hear his voice, the deep timbre of it vibrating with humor as he teased or flirted with her.

Derek shook his head, tousling his brown locks. After the divorce he'd started wearing his hair longer, probably to look younger. He did but that might have been due to his lack of responsibility more than his hairstyle. "No," he said, "it's easier for you to do the shopping for the kids."

Yes, easier for *him*…because he didn't have to do a damn thing. Just like when they were married. And just like when they were married, it was easier to do everything herself than argue with him to do it. She bit back a sigh and nodded. "Sure…"

He leaned closer and pressed a kiss to her forehead. "You're the best, Maggie." His brown eyes gleamed. "You've always been the best."

Despite her annoyance with him, a smile tugged at her lips. She knew that he was referring to something other than her cooking or shopping now. But his compliment was more over his fear of being alone than realizing how great she was. "Forget about it, Derek. It's not going to happen." Even if he was her secret Santa.

"You're a hard woman, Maggie O'Brien."

"Don't forget that."

Knuckles rapped against the metal edge of her fabric partition. "Am I interrupting?"

Maggie glanced up to meet her boss's gaze. If he'd really needed her, he would have buzzed her on the intercom…or yelled from his office. She couldn't imagine why he hadn't. "Not at all, you pay me. He doesn't."

"I pay, I pay," Derek insisted as he slid off the

corner of her desk. For once he reached for his wallet. "How much do you need to buy the kids' gifts for me to give them?"

She should take his money but use it to buy her own presents. "Did you look at their lists? They have expensive tastes." She glanced at Hal; a frown puckered his brow. "But we'll talk about that later. I'm working."

She couldn't set her own hours as Derek did; he worked in sales for a glass company. He "called" often on insurance companies, trying to win their business for replacement windshields and other vehicular glass. In fact, he'd found out Hal was looking for office help and had set up Maggie's interview seven years ago. Hal and Derek were friends.

"When are you going to play racquetball with me and Patrick?" Hal asked Derek. As well as being his client, Patrick was also Hal's friend. That was why Hal had recommended Mallehan Service to fix Maggie's van when she'd gotten suspicious that the garage she'd previously been using was overcharging her.

"Mallehan?" Derek asked.

His name conjured an image of the mechanic, golden hair, bright blue eyes, to Maggie's mind. Her pulse quickened.

Hal nodded.

"You guys still playing racquetball?" He lifted his

gaze to the insurance agent's graying hair. "You're not getting too old for that?"

Hal's gaze dropped to Derek's waist, where his white dress shirt pulled free of the strained waistband of his black pants. "Better than getting fat."

"Hey, someone call my name?" Patrick asked.

In greeting, Derek patted Mallehan's flat stomach. "Yeah, we were. We were talking about how you and Hal are getting old and fat."

Patrick flashed a grin at Maggie. "Sounds like a fascinating discussion for you. So what are you? The judge of which man's in the best shape?"

Maggie leaned back in her chair to study the three men standing around her desk. From the reception area drifted traditional Christmas music; it wasn't loud enough that Maggie could recognize the song because she'd made Constance, the receptionist, turn down the music. So she supplied her own words, "We Three Kings…"

She steepled her fingers under her chin. "Hmm… how should I judge this?"

Patrick had the muscular body of a blond Adonis. Hal, with his more pepper than salt hair, had a lean, runner's build. And Derek…he had the cuddly teddy-bear thing going for him that some women loved.

"How am I supposed to tell who's in the best shape?" she asked. An image flashed through her mind of the men stripped down to Speedos, walking in a circle around her desk.

Constance, the receptionist, leaned around the partition, her shoulder bumping against Patrick's arm. "Maggie, make them take off their shirts, so you can judge." She tilted her head to stare up at the sexy mechanic.

Maggie knew who had the vote of the blond receptionist. Maggie met Patrick's sparkling blue gaze. He had her vote, too. His wicked grin flashing, he reached for the buttons on his shirt, over which he wore his leather jacket open.

"Hey!" Hal protested, nudging Patrick off balance with his shoulder. "This is a place of business. Remember who's the boss here."

"Maggie's the boss," Constance said with a cocky grin before ducking back around the partition.

"Ain't that the truth," Derek said with a mock-weary sigh. "I'm getting out of here before you fools drag me off to racquetball."

"Scared we'll whip your butt?" Hal taunted him.

Derek wasn't the only boy of the three men. He grinned his dimpled grin. "I'm scared one of you big lugs will break a hip or blow out a knee and I'll have to carry you off the court."

Maggie shook her head. "If you guys don't dial down the testosterone, Constance and I may start burping and grunting, too."

On cue, a belch emanated from the reception area, followed by a giggle. Although less than a decade younger than Maggie, Constance sometimes acted quite immaturely. But then she didn't have the responsibility of three kids to support; she had only a cat.

"I'll walk you out, Derek," Hal said, steering his friend out of Maggie's office. "You're early for racquetball," he told Patrick.

"I'm dropping off Maggie's lemon."

"Another breakdown?" Hal asked her, as if it had been she and not the vehicle that had malfunctioned.

"I rig it to break down," Patrick said, his blue eyes sparkling with humor, "so that I have a reason to keep seeing her."

Hal and Derek both laughed, as if the thought of any man wanting to see Maggie was hilarious. She glared at them, but they missed her look of malice as they walked into the reception area.

"Wow, that was fast," she said of Patrick's repair job.

"I did it myself," he said but without conceit. "I did most of the job last night."

"Anything to avoid doing your paperwork, huh?" she teased.

"Something like that."

She reached for the handle of the deep bottom desk drawer where she kept her purse. "How much do I owe you for the…alternator?"

Patrick lifted his hand. "I didn't print out an invoice. I can bring that by later. I wanted to make sure you had a way to get home tonight."

Maggie's fingers tightened on the drawer pull. "Are you sure? Usually my check has to just about clear the bank before I can pick up the van."

Color tinged Patrick's cheeks. "That's Delilah's rule."

His secretary, Delilah, wasn't anything like her name implied. She was pushing sixty with a beehive of dyed black hair and a penetrating gaze. She was more protection for Mallehan's than a rottweiler.

"She's *my* boss," he said.

"If you don't get my check now, you're breaking her rule," Maggie warned him.

He shrugged. "I'm not worried about Delilah. I know my way around her."

His grin. His peppermint mochas. His smiling blue eyes. Maggie was afraid he might know his way around *her*, too.

"What about me?" she asked softly.

The others had walked farther out into the reception, their voices muffled as they spoke near the front door. She and Patrick were alone in her little corner.

"I'm not worried about your paying up…" he said as he walked all the way into her office. He rounded her desk and perched on the corner near her as Derek had. But, unlike Derek, Patrick's closeness unsettled her. His thigh, clad in snug denim, brushed against her arm. Heat radiated from his body, flushing her skin.

"I know where you live," he reminded her.

His tone, and the glint in his blue eyes, suggested that he knew more than her address. But he couldn't. Despite the number of years Maggie had worked for his friend, she hadn't met Patrick in person until she'd brought her van to him for the first time almost a year ago. He and Hal had always met outside the office, usually on a racquetball court or a golf course.

"What I don't know," he said, lowering his voice to a sexy rumble, "is what was in that little bag I found under your backseat."

She narrowed her eyes and stared hard at him even though she knew she couldn't break him the way she could her children. "Liar."

He leaned close and sniffed her hair. "Nice shampoo."

"It wasn't—" She caught herself before she revealed anything else.

He dipped his head further, and his soft hair brushed her cheek as he nuzzled her neck. "Perfume?"

Her heart slammed against her ribs. "Patrick!"

He didn't move away, his breath caressing her throat as he murmured, "Hmm…I wonder what it could be."

"Bubble bath," she admitted, fearful that he might keep nuzzling her neck and that she might do something stupid, like grab him and kiss him.

"So you used it already?" he asked as he drew back slightly.

"I was freezing," she said. Not that she'd had long to warm up with the kids coming home. She'd had to leave the bubbles in order to referee.

"And here I've always thought you were hot," he murmured as he leaned close again.

Heat flooded Maggie, raising her temperature and her desire. She caught herself leaning toward Patrick, but he pulled back and turned toward her wide doorway.

"You're popular today, Maggie," Hal said as he stepped back inside her partition.

She wasn't sure *what* she was today. Confused, mostly. Was Patrick interested or only playing with her? She didn't have time for games. Not his. Certainly not Derek's. And Hal…

After his wife had died a few years ago, she'd thought she could make time for Hal. He was good-looking. Smart. But nearly as helpless as Derek. She took care of him at work; she didn't need to take care of him at home, too.

"You needed something," she remembered, denying her own needs. Her desire…for Patrick Mallehan. She stood up and moved around her desk, via the corner opposite to which Patrick Mallehan sat, but her legs were shaky. It must have been from sitting so long. That had to be the reason. She needed to stretch.

"I can't get an e-mail open." Hal explained his problem. "Can you?"

She nodded. "I'll be there in a minute." She turned back to the man sitting yet on her desk. "Patrick…"

He waved her off. "Go ahead and help Hal. I don't want him to have any excuse for not playing well on the court today."

"Thank you for dropping off the van," she said. Why had he? To avoid his dreaded paperwork or because he wanted to see her? Could he be her secret Santa? "Make sure you get me that invoice."

"Delilah'll take care of that," he promised.

"I'm sure she will."

Was he like Derek and Hal? Did he need someone to take care of him? She considered the question when she returned to her now-deserted desk.

She'd opened up Hal's attachment with one click of the mouse. His daughter's Christmas list. Like Maggie, he had one in college. But he only had the one, whom he spoiled rotten. "I hope you can find everything on her list," he'd told Maggie, just assuming she'd handle the chore.

Just as with Derek, she hadn't been able to get out of doing his Christmas shopping, either. She dropped into her chair, then pulled open the bottom drawer of her desk, intent on putting Skylar's list in her purse. But she couldn't see her purse in the drawer for the gift bag covering it. This bag, in metallic green, was bigger than last night's.

Hands shaking, she drew the top apart and peeked inside. Green silk spilled out, so she lifted it.

"Someone's been to Victoria's Secret," Constance said, whistling softly in admiration of the gown Maggie held. "Did Hal give you a raise?"

Maggie shook her head. "I didn't buy it."

"Who did?"

She reached inside the bag for the card, which didn't address her by name. But this time she didn't doubt it was meant for her. "My secret Santa," she told Constance. She read his message silently. "'Feel like a woman.'"

THE GOWN had made her feel like a woman, for the little while she'd worn it before coming out tonight. This morning. This ungodly hour somewhere between Saturday night and Sunday morning. She stood in the Best Buy parking lot, in a line of other desperate people hoping to score the hot gift on every child's and some adults' wish lists.

If only Brandon didn't still believe in Santa Claus, she might not have been as desperate, desperate enough to risk pneumonia to get the one and only thing he'd put on his list. Sometimes she couldn't help disappointing her children, but she didn't want to disillusion them.

They had plenty of time to learn how tough life could be. While at ten Brandon was kind of old to still believe, she was glad that he did. She didn't want to lose her baby yet. Sometimes she wished *she* could still believe in Santa, too.

But no little man in a red suit had been bringing her presents. Who had bought her such personal gifts? She thought again of the green gown, felt the silken brush of it against her naked skin. Her nipples had pressed tightly against the fabric. She bit her lip, remembering how sensitive she'd been to the silk.

As Constance had pointed out, her secret Santa had to be one of the three wise guys who'd been in her office that day. Derek had been alone at her desk while she'd helped a client in the reception area. But could it be Derek, who refused to shop for his kids?

Hal had had a number of opportunities throughout the morning to get into her desk. But was it Hal, a man who wouldn't shop for his own daughter?

Or Patrick, who hadn't left immediately when she'd gone into Hal's office to retrieve that e-mail attachment. Did Patrick do his own shopping or leave that in Delilah's capable hands?

"Maggie!"

Recognition of the deep voice and realization washed over her simultaneously. Patrick Mallehan did his own shopping. He stood closer to the front of the line than she did—at least fifty people ahead of her. He waved his arm, gesturing her forward. "Honey, come on up here. She's my wife," he lied to the people between them. "We're together."

Although they grumbled, no one stopped her from moving up in line to stand next to Patrick, who slung an arm around her shoulders. "Hey, honey, you finally got out of bed to join me."

She would have pulled back, but she didn't want the other early-morning shoppers to know Patrick lied. They might riot. Also, he was warm while she, even bundled up in a parka, was not. She snuggled a bit closer.

"Good thing you're wearing gloves now," he said as he took her hand in his.

Some of the other shoppers began caroling, off-key, so she could speak freely. No one would hear her and Patrick talking above the chorus of "Grandma Got Run Over by a Reindeer."

"The kids are with Derek this weekend, and Kirsten, apparently, forgot to take my gloves." Instead of enjoying her time off from being just Mom by sinking deep into a warm bubble bath and lounging in bed in her new, silky nightgown, she'd spent the time shopping.

"How's the van running?"

"Great." She'd given it quite the workout this weekend. "I haven't gotten my invoice yet."

Patrick shook his head. "Delilah must be slipping."

Maybe off her chain, but that guard dog of a secretary wouldn't miss collecting any money for Mallehan's...unless Patrick had told her to forget about it.

"I want to pay you," she insisted.

"Make me some Christmas cookies," he said, reminding her, "I love sweets..."

His blue eyes flashed as he stared down at her in the same way she stared at a plate of dark chocolate fudge, with hunger and the knowledge that she'd probably regret giving in to temptation. Patrick Mallehan wasn't just a flirt or a successful businessman; there was much more to him.

"So tell me," she said, "why you're standing here in line." From Hal she'd learned Patrick was long-divorced, but she didn't know much else of a personal nature about him.

He sighed, his breath a white cloud in the cold pre-dawn air. "If I tell you, you're probably going to look at me differently."

A smile teased Maggie's lips. He was just like Hal and Derek, more boy than man. "So you're a *gamer*," she said, using Brandon's name for himself.

He chuckled. "Oh, I get sucked into a game from time to time, but the real gamer in my family is my grandson. His Christmas list is the reason I'm standing in line at this ungodly hour."

She sucked in a breath of frigid air. "You have a grandson?"

He nodded. "And now that you know I'm a grandpa, you're going to look at me differently."

"Hmm…you may be right." Now he was even sexier.

"I swear my teeth and hair are really mine."

"I know." She'd touched his hair, which had been softer than the nightgown from her secret Santa. How would that feel against her skin? Not just her cheek, which he'd brushed against in the office, but her throat, her breast…

She pushed the thought aside and asked, "So how'd you get standing-in-line duty and not his parents?"

"His mother's pregnant with his little sister." For a second his eyes brightened but then dimmed when he added, "and my son is in Iraq."

She squeezed his hand. "I'm sorry."

"It's his second tour. He'd only been home a little while before they called him back." Patrick pulled his hand from hers to rub it over his face.

"You didn't want him to join the service?"

Patrick shook his head. "No, but he wouldn't

listen to me. I didn't really expect him to. I wasn't always the greatest role model for my son."

"Patrick Mallehan, I can't believe you'd say that. You're so successful—"

"As a businessman, not a father." He sighed.

"I'm sure you have your reasons," she defended him, to him. She had no idea why she felt so strongly that he was being much too hard on himself. "You were probably working long hours, trying to make a success of the garage."

"I was working on growing up. I was just a teenager when I became a father."

"Really?"

"Same old story. Dumb jock knocks up head cheerleader. Instead of using his college scholarship, he has to support his wife and kid so goes to work as a mechanic. My dad was a shop teacher who worked on cars on the weekend. He taught me a lot…when I bothered to listen to him. I was a huge disappointment to my father," he said the last as if warning her that he might disappoint her, too.

Somehow she doubted that. She'd learned long ago to have no expectations. But still she defended him. "I'm sure you're being too hard on yourself. Look at you now."

He shook his head. "I set a horrible example for my son. He wound up doing the same thing I did, knocking up his high-school sweetheart. But even though he repeated one of my mistakes, he's a lot smarter than me. He picked a sweet girl. He and Linda are happy…when he's home. He's a good man and a much better father than I ever was."

"Patrick…"

He shrugged his shoulders. "Don't feel sorry for me. I can't redo the past, but I'm going to do that thing so many other men do. Be a better grandfather than I was a father. I'm going to make sure Justin gets everything he wants for Christmas."

A shout went up from the crowd as the store doors slid open. "Our shipment's here," a manager called out, "but we only got in five game systems. And because we don't know when we're getting another shipment, we can't give out rain checks."

The crowd booed, then jockeyed for position, pushing toward the front. Patrick tightened his arm around Maggie's shoulders and drew her back toward the parking lot. "There are a lot more than five people in front of us."

Disappointment settled heavily on her heart. "We're not going to get the game system."

"Not this time," Patrick agreed.

"I'm sorry." She was more disappointed for Patrick than herself.

He tucked her close to his side. "It's okay. It's not what Justin really wants. He's just so smart, even at eight, that he knows Santa can't bring him what he really wants."

"His father back home," Maggie said. "I think that's the only thing on your Christmas list, too, Patrick Mallehan."

They drew alongside her van, but before Maggie could open the door, he pulled her closer. "You'd be surprised what I have on my list, Maggie O'Brien."

Her? God, she wished she had time to be someone's Christmas present. But she still had gifts to get, cookies to bake—so much to do before the holidays.

She tugged loose. Maybe in the new year….

"Maggie…"

She busied herself finding her keys in her purse, not that she'd bothered to lock her doors. "Patrick, I'd like to…talk to you more…but I have so much to do…"

"Maggie," he said again. "You have something sitting in your backseat. Another gift bag. Where else were you shopping this morning?"

The sun had not even risen yet. She hadn't been anywhere else; she hadn't left a metallic gold gift bag in her backseat. Her secret Santa had struck again.

"I have to start locking my doors," she murmured, as she knelt on the driver's seat and reached for the bag.

"So what is it?"

Secret Santa had gotten a bit more creative. He'd

put tissue paper inside the bag with whatever gift he'd given her. She had to take the present out and unwrap the red sparkling paper. When she uncovered the gift, heat rushed into her face. "Oh—"

"What is it?" Patrick asked again, leaning into the driver's door.

She tried to push it back into the bag, but she wasn't fast enough.

He chuckled. "Well, your secret admirer is a pervert."

"Maybe it's a gag," she said, defending the man who'd given her the sweet scented lotions and silky nightgown. She reached inside the bag and drew out the envelope containing the small card. She opened the card and read the message to herself. Take pleasure in being a woman.

She glanced again to the gift, a ribbed vibrator. She'd thought about buying one, but she'd never found the courage to go to a store that would carry such items. She couldn't have mail-ordered it, either, and risked having one of the kids getting the mail and opening her little toy.

She'd heard other women brag about not needing a man as long as they had enough batteries. Could it really bring that much pleasure? She stared at the toy, secretly fascinated. Then she glanced up at Patrick, whose blue eyes were intent on her face, studying her.

Could it bring her as much pleasure as he could?

Somehow she doubted it. *Take pleasure in being a woman*. He was the only man who treated her as if she was a woman, and not his mother. Should she take her secret Santa's advice but with Patrick and not the toy?

CHAPTER 3

"All I Want For Christmas…"

"I really should be shopping," Maggie said, reminding herself, as she perched on a stool in Patrick Mallehan's kitchen. She should be doing anything other than what she was considering.

His kitchen was the antithesis of hers with all-white cabinets and stainless-steel appliances. Instead of country it looked commercial but with just enough touches—like the silvery granite and gray-blue walls—to add warmth.

"It's still early," Patrick pointed out, gesturing toward the window in which the first, faint gray light of the December morning shone. "Most of the stores are still closed."

Maggie couldn't believe she'd awakened so early to stand in line in the frigid cold. She wrapped her hands tighter around the mug Patrick refilled with cinnamon-flavored coffee. "Only five game systems.

I can't believe that was all they could get even though they put an ad in the paper."

"Well, they drew quite a crowd, so they got what they wanted."

"We didn't," she reminded him.

"I don't know," he said, "I have Maggie O'Brien alone in my house…."

"And that's what you want?" she asked.

"My house for starters."

"And next?" she persisted, wanting to know where he wanted them to go…even if she couldn't meet him there.

"My kitchen."

"The kitchen's good," she agreed, the sleek style growing on her. His food was better. Not only was he not helpless like Derek and Hal but he was very talented. She stuck her fork in what was left of the fluffy omelet Patrick had folded onto her plate. Cheese oozed out, spreading over green pepper, tomatoes and hash browns.

"Your cooking is better." She shouldn't have another bite, but she was tempted.

She lifted her gaze from her plate to focus on the cook. Patrick stood on the other side of the island, one palm braced on the silver granite countertop while he sipped some coffee. His throat, bared by his open-neck shirt, rippled as he swallowed. Patrick Mallehan was far more temptation than the omelet.

He drew the cup from his mouth and set it back on the counter. "I had more in mind than the kitchen."

"Patrick…"

He moved around the island and leaned over her. "Maggie, you can give me what's on my Christmas list."

"What's on your Christmas list, Patrick?" she asked, a smile stealing over her at the devilish gleam in his blue eyes. Her pulse raced as his head dipped toward hers.

"You, Maggie. You're on my Christmas list."

She reached up, cupping his face in her hands. Her lips touched his, just a soft, silky brush. "Well, since I can't get my son what he wants…"

"You'll give me what I want?" Patrick asked, his eyes brightening up like the kid on Christmas morning who actually finds what he wants under the tree.

Would Brandon?

She closed her eyes, unwilling to think about her kids or shopping. Or anything but Patrick as she waited for his kiss.

"What about you, Maggie?" he asked.

She blinked. "What?"

"What's on your Christmas list?"

Figuring what he expected her to say, she said, "You."

He laughed, his breath tickling her lips with the promise of the kiss for which she still waited. "Liar."

"Hmm…it's been a while for me, but I don't quite remember insults being part of foreplay."

"Why's it been a while for you, Maggie?" he persisted, still teasing her with his mouth so close to hers while all he did was talk. Well, actually, he was interrogating her.

She fought the smile that tugged at her lips. "I just haven't met the right man."

"Liar."

"I don't want to sound critical, but you could use a little work on your endearments, Patrick."

"I was straight with you," he reminded her. "I told you about myself."

"About your son. Why you were standing in line at Best Buy at the crack of dawn."

"What else is there to know?"

Warmth flooded her chest. He'd told her about what he considered most important: his family. How he felt he'd failed them and had to make up to them. But still she had questions. "You didn't tell me about your marriage or your divorce."

"Because my ex-wife doesn't matter. We weren't married very long."

So Patrick Mallehan had been on his own a long time. He had no fear of being alone.

"Does Derek matter to you?" he asked.

She shook her head. "I just don't want him dis-appointing my kids." That was her job.

"That's why you do his shopping for them?"

She nodded.

"So why do you do Hal's?"

She shrugged. "He's my boss."

"Is that all?"

She laughed. "Are you the possessive type?"

"No," he said with believable sincerity. "I'm just trying to understand you, Maggie O'Brien. I'm trying to understand why it's 'been a while' for a beautiful woman like you."

"Because most of the time I'm *not* a woman." She sighed, weary from more than just lack of sleep. "I'm a mother, an ex-wife, an office manager…"

He pressed his finger to her lips, stemming her flow of job descriptions. "You're *always* a woman, Maggie."

He had to be her secret Santa. He had to be….

"Sometimes I forget," she admitted.

"Then let me remind you…."

He kissed her then. Finally. A real kiss with lips and teeth and tongues. A kiss that reminded Maggie of backseats and dark movie theatres and secluded park benches. But Patrick didn't kiss like anyone in her memories. He didn't kiss like a boy; he kissed like a man with skill and control. She was the one who lost control, whose hormones overwhelmed her common sense…like when she was twenty…or younger.

Her pulse raced and her breath shuddered in her lungs. She reached for his hair first, delving her fingers into the silken strands. Then she skimmed her hands down his nape to his shoulders, to the breadth of muscle that shifted and bunched beneath her palms. "Patrick…"

He pulled back, his breathing ragged, his pupils enlarged so that only a thin circle of blue rimmed the black. "Maggie, we can stop—"

"I don't want to stop," she told him.

He swung her up in his arms as easily as if she weighed what an alternator weighed…whatever an alternator was. She slid her arm around his neck, holding on, scared that she might fall and not just to the floor.

He turned sideways to carry her through a doorway. Then he dropped his arm from beneath her legs so that she slid down his body, which was all hard, taut muscle.

"Patrick…" She wrapped her arms around him, expecting him to disappear, expecting to awaken from a dream. This couldn't be real. He couldn't be real.

He dipped his head and kissed her again, his mouth moving over hers, parting her lips, his tongue sliding inside to tempt and taste and tease. Her lungs strained for breath, but she didn't care. She didn't need to breathe as long as he kept kissing her. Kept touching her.

His hands moved slowly and softly, first over her face as if he were blind and trying to memorize every feature. He traced her brows, her cheekbones, her jaw. Then his fingers skimmed down her throat, over her madly pounding pulse to her collarbone.

Earlier she'd unzipped her sweatshirt because she'd been warm in his house, in his presence. The blue knit dropped to the floor as he pushed it from her shoulders. Then he toyed with the spaghetti straps of the pink tank top she wore with faded jeans. He lifted his head, pulling away from their kiss to study her with a hot gaze.

Fingers trembling slightly, she reached for the buttons on his shirt. It had been so long since she'd undressed a man. Maybe she never had. She parted his shirt to a wall of muscle, lightly dusted with golden hair.

"Damn, you're in good shape," she murmured. Would he be disappointed that she wasn't? That she had more curves than muscles?

"You're so beautiful," he groaned as he leaned down to kiss her bare shoulder.

Maggie shivered at the brush of his mouth against her skin. Then he lifted up her tank top and pulled it off over her head. Because of its built-in bra, she wore nothing beneath.

He exhaled a ragged breath. "Maggie…"

Exposed, vulnerable, she wrapped her arms around him again, pressing her chest to his. Her nipples, hard and sensitive, pushed against his warm skin and soft hair. His hands slid over her bare back.

"Don't be shy," he teased her.

"It's been a while," she reminded him.

"I want to see you," he said, "lying naked on my bed. In my arms."

"Is that on your Christmas list?"

He nodded, his eyes gleaming with mischief and desire.

She dragged in a deep breath, then stepped back. As she did, she reached for the snap of her jeans. In for a penny… She discarded her jeans and the thin pair of cotton panties she'd worn beneath them.

"Oh, Maggie," he groaned.

She walked to his bed and draped herself across the navy-blue comforter. "Here's your early Christmas present then."

"Merry Christmas to me," he murmured as he shouldered off his open shirt, then tore open his belt and dropped his jeans. His erection strained against his briefs, which he quickly dropped.

Damn. He was big. Much, much bigger than her battery-operated Christmas present. "Patrick…"

"Don't change your mind now," he implored her, obviously picking up on her nervousness.

"No, I'm not changing my mind. You can't take back Christmas presents."

He dropped onto the bed with her, braced on his elbows so that only his lower half touched hers. His penis nudged, hot and hard, against her hip. The hair on his legs tickled hers. "And I'm not letting you go."

But he was. He was letting her go. He was letting her lose control, letting her take time for herself, making her remember that she was a woman. Always.

"Now I remember what's on my list," she murmured as she skimmed her lips across his shoulder.

"Am I really there?" he asked.

She closed her eyes and sighed, "Oh, yes…" He was right up there with time for herself. Like this. She needed more time like this.

"You haven't started without me, have you?" he murmured as his mouth moved along her shoulder. Then his hair brushed away his kisses as he moved along. He nibbled his way across her breast until his lips closed over her nipple, tugging and suckling.

"Oh, yes," she murmured again as heat flooded her, pulsing between her legs, which she wrapped around him.

"Slow down," he said. "I want to take my time with you."

Time. That was all she wanted. And this. More of both. But she couldn't slow down. His kisses ignited her passion. She squirmed against the brushed suede comforter as he suckled one breast and teased the other with his fingers.

"Oh…" A little orgasm spilled from her.

Patrick groaned. "Damn, you're hot," he murmured as he slid a finger inside her. "So hot…" He kept stroking her until she came again.

"Patrick!"

"Shhh…there's more," he promised her. So much more. First he showed her with his mouth, moving his lips and tongue between her legs. Torturing her until she sobbed out an explosive orgasm. Then he sheathed his pulsing erection and pushed inside her, filling her deeper than she'd ever been filled.

She wrapped her legs and arms around him, holding tight, matching his thrusts with her hips, pulling him deep with her muscles until she came again, shattering in his arms. The cords in his neck strained as he shouted his release.

He kept her clasped in his arms and rolled them until she lay on top of him. "Merry Christmas to me," he murmured.

Maggie pressed a kiss against Patrick's chest, slick with perspiration. "So admit it."

"What?"

"You're my secret Santa."

A chuckle rumbled in his chest. "Aren't you a little old to still believe in Santa Claus?"

"Secret admirer then?"

"There's nothing secret about my admiration for you, Maggie. I think you're wonderful. Beautiful. Sexy. Strong. Independent."

"I'm glad you consider that a compliment," she said.

"Beauty? Sexiness? Strength?"

"Independence." Maybe he wouldn't expect every minute of her time and attention just because they'd slept together. She didn't have much time and attention to spare.

He sighed. "I'll have Delilah get the invoice together for the alternator."

"Well, good, I want to pay you." But he'd mistaken what she'd meant by her vow of independence. She hadn't meant just that she could take care of herself; she meant that she wouldn't be taking care of him, too.

"You weren't talking about the alternator," he realized.

"No." She drew back and pulled a corner of the navy-blue comforter tight to her breasts. "I don't really have time for this."

"This?" he asked, sitting up against the mahogany headboard so that he studied her, his blue eyes intense.

"Us." Heat rushed into her face. Was she wrong in assuming that he wanted more from her than what they'd just done? "I don't know if that's what you want. I'm just saying that I don't have time for a relationship. With anyone."

"Not even your secret Santa?"

She narrowed her eyes. "So it is you?"

He shook his head. "How smart would I be if I bought you something so that you don't need me?"

"What? Oh…" The vibrator. "I don't have time for that either, Patrick. My life is so busy."

He nodded. "I've noticed that. You take a lot upon yourself."

Too much. Too many other people's responsibilities. "You're right."

"You need to make sure you save some time for yourself."

And what about him? How much of her time did he want?

"I'll be here," he said, "if you want to spend some of that time with me."

He didn't demand or plead. He only offered. Relief lifted her heart; desire prodded it to beat harder. Faster.

"The holidays are crazy."

"I know." He reached out and brushed a stray red curl behind her ear. His touch lingered on the curve of her jaw. "Thank you for my early Christmas present, Maggie O'Brien."

Her breath shuddered out with the admission: "It

was great." More than great. Amazing. Awesome. Beyond anything she'd ever experienced before.

"Just great?" Patrick said, his eyes darkening as if offended. Then his wicked grin flashed, and he reached for her. "I'll show you great."

SO MAYBE she would have appreciated her last gift more…if she hadn't been with Patrick Mallehan. After him the vibrator didn't fascinate her as much. Only Patrick fascinated her. She'd learned so much about him that night—morning, but there was so much she needed to learn.

About him and about herself. After the divorce, she'd thought she'd finally found herself, but she'd lost so much of herself, too. Because she'd concentrated on being a mom and an office manager and an ex-wife, she'd forgotten she was a woman, too. She'd found that part of herself in Patrick's arms.

But for more than a week, she'd had to put the woman on hold. She'd had to bake and shop, and still she hadn't tracked down all the gifts on her kids' lists.

"So I'm not buying yours," she told Derek, who sat in his usual spot on the corner of her desk, leaning over her.

"What?" he asked as he played with her Rolodex, spinning the wheel of business cards, just like Brandon did whenever he came to the office.

"I can't find everything *I* want to get the kids, so I'm not doing your shopping, too." She handed him back the money he'd dropped on her desk.

"Maggie…" He stared at her, trying to suck her in with his puppy-dog eyes.

She was so over puppies and little boys. "No, Derek, we've been divorced for six years. I'm not doing your shopping anymore. You need to do this yourself, for yourself and the kids. A gift from you will mean more to them when they know you actually picked it out."

"You're different," Derek said, his eyes narrowing. "What's going on with you?"

"Nothing." Because she didn't have the time. For Patrick. Or herself. Santa had brought her some great gifts, but he hadn't given her the most important thing on her list.

"That's your problem then," Derek said as if making an important discovery. "You're frustrated."

She nodded. "Yes, frustrated with the men in my life who don't realize I have a life. That I'm not dying to take care of them, to run their errands, do their shopping—"

"Okay," Derek interrupted, holding his hands up as if to ward off her attack. "I understand. You don't want to do the shopping. I thought you were playing before, but I guess you really are a Scrooge, Maggie O'Brien."

She shook her head. "Actually, for the first time in

a long time, I'm enjoying Christmas." Because for once she wasn't doing all the giving; she was receiving, too.

"You're not going to tell me what's going on with you," Derek realized. He always told her everything, about his job, about the women he dated, because he loved to talk about himself.

Maggie smiled as she shook her head. "We're not married anymore," she reminded him.

"No, but I thought we were friends."

While they'd stayed friendly for the sake of the kids, she and Derek had never really been friends. Were he and Patrick friends? Would things be strange between them if she were ever to have more than those stolen hours with Patrick? Then she reminded herself of what she'd just reminded Derek. They weren't married anymore. They weren't even friends. She didn't care what he thought of her seeing Patrick. She didn't even care what the kids thought of her dating.

She had to work out how *she* felt about her dating again. And about Patrick. Did she want to make time for him when she hadn't yet figured out how to make it for herself?

"Maggie, you have a call on line two," Constance called out from the reception area.

"I have to take this," she told her ex, even though she wasn't sure there was actually a person on the phone. She often had Constance interrupt Derek's little visits. He took his time standing up and walking away from her. Just in case she actually had a caller, she picked up the phone. "Maggie O'Brien."

"Hello, Maggie O'Brien."

Warmth flooded her heart. "Hello, Patrick Mallehan. I got my invoice from Delilah."

"That's good. I'll be able to make next month's mortgage payment."

"Not from this. You only charged me for the part and that was at your cost. I checked with Delilah." Because she hadn't believed the rottweiler would have made a mistake on the bill. She hadn't; she'd only been following her boss's orders.

"I couldn't charge you for labor. Some broken-down old mechanic worked on it."

Her smile widened. "*You* did." And she knew for a fact he wasn't broken-down or old.

"Yes, I did."

Her vehicle wasn't all he'd worked on for her. "So why are you calling?"

For a date? A real date? And what was she going to do if he asked? She had no time now. But how long could she put him off without his losing interest?

"Can you take a break right now?"

"I'm at work," she pointed out.

"Yeah, I know, but you're the boss," he reminded her. "Even Hal says so."

"But we're really busy right now—" Too busy for her to skip out for a hot date; regret nagged at her.

"Come on, Maggie, I can't hold on to this much longer."

"Jeez, Patrick." She couldn't believe that he expected her to drop everything for, in Kirsten's words, a booty call. He was just like the other men she knew: a self-centered little boy. "I think you got the wrong idea—"

"You already got the game system?"

Confusion furrowed her forehead. "No. But what does that have to do—"

"I kept stopping by the store, hoping I'd catch them just as they were getting another shipment. I did. I'm holding on to two of the systems right now, but they'll only let me buy one," he explained, then he lowered his voice to an urgent whisper, "Get down to the Best Buy on Alpine before the mob overpowers me."

She grabbed her purse out of her bottom drawer. "I'll be right there."

"Where are you going?" Hal asked as she hung up the phone and vaulted out of her chair.

Maggie passed him in the doorway. "I have a Christmas shopping emergency."

"I thought you were sick of shopping," he said.

He'd obviously overheard her argument with Derek. "Sick of other people's," she clarified, referring to her ex.

"Then forget about doing mine."

"What?" She hadn't meant to offend her boss. "I didn't—" God, she didn't have time for another argument.

"No, that's okay," he assured her. "I wasn't thinking about how much else you have to do, being a single mom, when I asked you."

He'd never really asked. That first Christmas after his wife died, she'd offered…out of pity, and every year since he'd just assumed. "Hal, we can talk about this later. I really have to go. I'll be right back."

Unless she made a side trip back to Patrick's house to thank him for scoring the game system for her. Not only did Patrick Mallehan do his own shopping but he'd done hers, too.

"You have that appointment with the Stephensons at three," Constance reminded her as she headed for the door. Then she lowered her voice to a whisper. "And thanks a lot."

"For what?"

"I'm doing Hal's shopping now."

"Did Derek ask you, too?"

She nodded, then laughed. "But since I don't work for him, I could say no." She shook her head. "Now I remember why I live with a cat."

And not a man. Constance hadn't learned what Maggie had; not all men were little boys.

CHAPTER 4

"Joy to the World…"

Maggie turned up the Christmas music and settled into a corner of the couch, her hands wrapped around a mug of fresh coffee. The only lights in the house twinkled, like myriad colored stars, on the Christmas tree in the middle of the family room. The lights reflected off the bright metallic paper of the presents stacked beneath the tree. The kids, when they finally awakened, would find Santa had brought them nearly everything on their lists. Maggie would probably still be paying off her credit card next Christmas.

Santa hadn't brought her what she wanted. She only had time for herself now because she'd set her alarm for five o'clock, knowing not even Brandon would be up that early. They'd gone to midnight Mass, but even though she hadn't had much sleep, Maggie wasn't tired. Perhaps it had something to do with the three cups of coffee she'd consumed before settling onto the warm plaid couch with her fourth. Or perhaps it was the excitement building in her that dispelled her weariness. Christmas was nearly over; she'd have more time then. For herself. And maybe for Patrick Mallehan.

Now she wondered what she'd really wanted most from Santa. Time? Or Patrick Mallehan naked under her tree with just a bow around his…

"Mom!" Brandon shouted down the hall as he burst into the family room, his eyes wide with some of the excitement she felt. "Mom! It's Christmas!"

"I know, honey," she chuckled.

He hadn't even noticed her sitting on the couch. He was totally focused on the tree and the mountain of presents beneath it. He'd only had one thing on his list, but she'd gotten him a few more presents. Socks. Underwear. The kinds of things kids hate getting for Christmas, but she'd needed to even out the present count between him and his siblings. They kept track.

"Shut up, bigmouth," Kirsten griped as she stumbled into the room, her big green eyes bleary with sleep, her red hair tousled around her shoulders. She was such a lovely girl on the outside, but sometimes she could be a spoiled brat. As the only girl, she'd always be the "princess" of the family.

"Did you wake up your brother?" Maggie asked her daughter. As an athlete, Cody expended so much energy when awake that he slept like the dead; it took far more than Brandon's shouting to awaken him.

An evil gleam lit Kirsten's eyes. "Oh, yes, I woke Cody up."

"I'm going to kill her," the teenager grumbled as he walked into the room. Water dripped from his nose, chin and brown curls.

"Merry Christmas!" Maggie greeted her children. She set her mug on the end table and stood to hug each squirming child.

"Mom?" Kirsten asked, as if checking Maggie's identity, while she pulled away from her embrace.

Maggie hugged her children but apparently not enough that they didn't grow suspicious of her affection. Did they think she hadn't gotten them any of the items on their lists? Or were they taken aback that she no longer played the Scrooge?

"Can we open presents now?" Brandon asked, his fingers already playing with a corner of the paper on his "special" gift.

"There's hot chocolate and warm muffins in the kitchen," she told them.

Cody's stomach growled like a dog before attacking. He grinned and said, "Sounds good to me."

"I'll get it," Maggie offered. She was only gone a few minutes, but by the time she walked back into the family room most of the paper had been torn from the presents and tossed around the Berber carpet.

"Thanks!" Kirsten said, holding up a ridiculously overpriced name-brand hoodie. "I love it!"

The memory of going into the store, and being dismissed by the salesclerks for not being a size 2 or less, flashed through Maggie's mind. That hooded sweatshirt had been nearly as hard to purchase as Brandon's game system.

"Me, too, Mom," Cody said as he pulled a Red Wings hockey jersey over his wet head.

Had they blown it? Had Brandon picked up that they were thanking her, not Santa? He lifted his gaze from the game in his lap, his brown eyes bright with unshed tears. Not tears of disillusionment or disappointment but tears of sheer joy. "Thanks, Mom!"

Her little boy didn't believe in Santa anymore. He believed in *her*. She blinked at the tears gathering in her eyes and said a quick, silent thanks to Patrick Mallehan for finding the game system.

Patrick. Every thought circled back to him.

"There're no gifts from Dad this year," Kirsten said, her green eyes intent. As the oldest she still harbored some resentment over the divorce. Despite Maggie being the one who'd filed, her loyal daughter had always remained firmly on her side. Maybe she wasn't such a brat.

"He's bringing your presents himself," Maggie shared.

"Dad shopped?" Cody asked, chuckling.

Kirsten pulled her pretty mouth into a petulant grimace. "We're not going to get what we want."

"We already did," Brandon pointed out, reaching for the cup of cocoa Maggie held out to him.

She'd just distributed the mugs and muffins from the tray when the doorbell rang. "It's early yet. Who could it be?" Her hand shook as she set the tray down and headed for the door. Everything kept coming back to Patrick Mallehan.

But when she opened the door, the man standing before her wore a red velvet coat, pants and stocking cap. Snowflakes drifted down, sparkling as they landed on his coat and hat. "Ho, ho, ho!"

She swallowed a groan. No, not…

"Dad!" Brandon said as he joined her in the hall. He hurled himself at his father. "You came for Christmas."

She hoped that was the only reason, for their kids, not for her. Derek could *not* be her secret Santa. But he'd shopped for the kids; he carried a big red bag of presents, knocking it against the doorjamb as he stepped inside the house. Shivering, Maggie slammed the door behind him to shut out the cold.

"Merry Christmas to you, too, Maggie," Derek murmured. "I didn't think you'd mind my stopping by this morning."

"I don't mind." She just wished he were someone else. Maggie swallowed a sigh of disappointment as she followed her ex and Brandon into the family room.

"Hey, Daddy," Kirsten said, raising her voice to the high-pitched tone of a little girl. "What'd you bring me?"

Derek chuckled. "Santa will give out the presents as soon as he gets some milk and cookies." He glanced down at the mugs of hot chocolate and plates of muffins on the coffee table. "Or whatever you have."

Maggie patted his belly in the red suit. "You don't need any more padding. Oh, that's not padding…" Maybe he *should* have gone to racquetball with Hal and Patrick. But then they might have had to carry *him* off the court.

"Cute," Derek murmured around the bite of muffin he'd stolen from Brandon's plate. "Umm… chocolate chip."

"My favorite," Cody said, popping the last of his muffin in his mouth before his father could steal any more than crumbs.

"Mom got us everything we wanted," Kirsten goaded Derek. "What did you get us?" Her tone, sharp with sass, implied something they didn't want.

Maggie would have intervened if Derek deserved the help. She'd divorced him; she hadn't sued him for full custody. She hadn't kept him from his kids;

he had. When he was dating someone, he cancelled weekends with them. He forgot birthdays. He didn't come to school events. Since this was the first year he'd ever bought presents, that he'd ever bought anything for the kids, she hoped he'd done good.

Derek's hand, shaking slightly, fumbled with the mouth of the big, red velvet satchel. His dark eyes glowed with the same excitement of his ten-year-old when Brandon had spotted all the presents under the tree.

"These things weren't on your lists," he admitted. But from the gleam of excitement in his eyes, he was pretty sure they would like them anyway.

Pity panged Maggie's heart. She'd learned the hard way not to stray from the list beyond the token gifts of socks and underwear. They expected those. But giving them anything they didn't want led to disappointment for everyone involved. Poor Derek. He'd tried…

"Dad!" Kirsten exclaimed.

"Cool!" Cody shouted.

Brandon added an awed, "Wow…"

Maggie peered around Derek to the snowboards he'd pulled from his bag. "I didn't wrap them," he said, "I didn't have any fancy paper."

The children didn't care, and neither did Maggie since she had enough torn remnants of fancy paper to pick up from the floor.

"Mom, can you take us up to Boyne Mountain?" Cody asked. "I want to try out my new board."

"That's mine," Kirsten said, pulling the purple board from her brother's hands. "Can we go up north, Mom?"

Brandon didn't add a plea to his siblings'. He widened his big dark eyes and stared up at her, knowing his begging-puppy-dog impersonation still got to her.

Damn Derek. Despite buying the gifts himself, he'd nevertheless made more work for her.

"There's one more thing in the bag," Derek said, reaching inside to pull something from the bottom of the red satchel.

God, she hoped it wasn't something for her. She didn't want Derek to be her secret Santa. She wanted Patrick.

"Plane tickets!" Kirsten shrieked when she recognized the envelope. "Daddy!" She dropped the board to throw her arms around her father's neck. "Where are we going?"

"Aspen. Sheila, the travel agent, swore it's the best place for snowboarding."

"Cool!" Cody shouted.

"Do you mind, Maggie?" Derek asked, trying his puppy dog eyes on her. No doubt he realized, too late, that he should have asked her first before making travel plans for her children. "They have this whole week off from school, right?"

The second week of their Christmas vacation. Another week of constant bickering.

"Is Mom going, too?" Brandon asked, not nearly as excited as the older kids.

"I can get you a ticket," Derek offered. "If you want to come."

She had a feeling he wanted an excuse to go back to the travel agent. He probably wanted to date her. She preferred his wanting to date Sheila rather than Maggie herself. She shook her head. "No, you should have run this past me first, but it's fine. I told you to buy their presents yourself."

"You did great, Daddy," Kirsten said.

"Didn't you get Mom anything?" Brandon asked.

Derek's face flushed as red as his suit. "I didn't think—"

"He gave me something," Maggie assured her son. He'd given her time alone. Before she could ponder what she was going to do with it, the phone rang. As she reached for it, her hand trembled the way Derek's had as he'd opened the gift bag. Her caller *had* to be Patrick, probably wondering if Brandon was as excited about the game system as Justin had been. Brandon had been thrilled before Derek had outdone her. "Hello?"

"Maggie?"

Disappointment dashed away her excitement. "Hal?" Her boss was helpless and dependent on her, but even he didn't bother her on holidays.

"Merry Christmas, Maggie."

"Merry Christmas," she parroted back. "Hal, is there something you need—"

"I realize I've been taking advantage of you, Maggie," Hal admitted with a heavy sigh. "So Connie and I came up with the perfect apology."

Connie? "Constance?"

The receptionist's voice rang out in the background of Hal's call. "Tell Maggie Merry Christmas."

"You don't need to apologize," she insisted.

"Well, reward you then. I'm giving you this week off, Maggie. Connie and I can handle the office. Since it's always slow during the holidays, we won't even call you. Enjoy your time off. We'll see you next year."

Constance and Hal? Just what had she bought his daughter for Christmas? "Thank you," she murmured, then replaced the receiver.

Maggie had been given the gift of more time. But it stretched out long and lonely before her. She would have preferred Patrick Mallehan naked beneath her tree. She had to stop thinking about him. No doubt he was with his family, his daughter-in-law and grandson, missing his son. Her heart shifted, hurting for him. But Patrick was strong and independent. He didn't need her.

After she helped them pack and dropped her kids and Derek at the airport, no one needed her…for an entire week.

SHE'D WASHED the dishes from Christmas dinner and picked up all the torn paper. Now she was back where she'd begun the day at 5:00 a.m., sitting on the couch in the family room, staring at the twinkling lights on the Christmas tree. But her skin was soft from her long bubble bath, her muscles relaxed. She shifted against the cushions, and the silk nightgown moved with her, caressing her.

Her breath shuddered out in a contented sigh. Well, nearly contented. She needed Santa to bring her one more gift. On cue the doorbell pealed. Her lips curved into a smile, she rose from the couch and walked down the hall. She didn't duck into her room for a robe. Everyone else had vowed to leave her alone; it could only be one person.

She opened the door and leaned against the jamb, uncaring of the cold night air and snow swirling around the man standing in front of her. Just the sight of his long, hard body in his black leather jacket, an open-neck black shirt and faded jeans, warmed her blood so that it pulsed through her throbbing body. The man was so *hot* she imagined the snow sizzling as flakes landed in his soft, blond hair. "Patrick Mallehan."

"Maggie O'Brien," he acknowledged her, his blue eyes gleaming with desire as his gaze skimmed up and down her body in the green gown. "Merry Christmas—"

She reached for him, fisted her hands in the lapels

of his black jacket and pulled him inside the house. After slamming the door shut with her hip, she rose on her toes and slanted her mouth across his. She kissed him hungrily, as though he was a double chocolate chip muffin and she was starving. Her lips clung to his while she pushed his jacket from his shoulders.

He tore his mouth away, his chest rising and falling with his harsh breathing. "Maggie—"

"We're alone," she said between pants. "Derek took the kids for a week."

"God, I feel so bad about that," he said, his eyes twinkling like the lights on the tree as he slid his hands over her. His palms glided down her back and over her silk-covered hips.

"You do?"

"Yeah, I didn't get him anything for Christmas." His fingers clutched the silk. "You're not wearing anything under this."

Maggie's heart pounded madly. "And you're wearing too much." She reached for the buttons on his shirt, scraping her nails across each inch of skin she exposed.

Patrick groaned. "You're bad…"

"You haven't seen anything yet," she promised him as she tugged his shirt free of his jeans. She slid her nails down his chest, over his washboard stomach to his belt. God, he was gorgeous. Her best Christmas present yet.

He caught her hand, stilling her fingers, but she

rested her palm on the erection straining against his fly. She taunted him, "You know you want me."

"Too much," he admitted with a groan. He dipped his head, but his lips missed her mouth, sliding across her cheek to her ear. He nipped at her lobe before skimming his mouth down her throat.

Goose bumps rose along Maggie's shoulders and arms as excitement tingled in every nerve. "Now who's bad?"

"You!" He groaned as she slid her palm up and down the denim-covered length of his erection. "You better be good, or Santa will bring you a lump of coal," he threatened her.

A smile lifted her lips. "Too late. Santa already brought me everything I wanted." Time. And Patrick Mallehan.

He leaned down, nuzzled her shoulder, then ran the tip of his tongue along her bare skin. "Mmm…" He ran his hands over her gown again, his hands lingering on the curve of her hips and the side of her breasts. "Oh, yeah, Santa has great taste."

She rose on her tiptoes to nip at his chin, then press her mouth to his. She slid her tongue between his lips. He tasted of coffee and peppermint. "Yes, he does…."

"So you don't want anything else from Santa?"

She ran her palms up his bare chest. His heart thumped against her hand. He wanted her as badly as she wanted him. A sense of power rushed over her, heady and exciting. "Oh, I want more from Santa. A whole lot more."

"Since you're waiting for the fat man in the red suit, should I get out of your way?" he teased.

The fat man in the red suit had already come to her house; he wasn't who she wanted. He was her past. She hoped Patrick would be her future, or at least a part of it. He wasn't going to admit it, but she refused to believe anyone but Patrick could be her secret Santa. Still dizzy with the sense of power, she tugged on his belt. "I want you to get out of your pants."

A deep chuckle shook his chest. But his laughter dissolved into a groan when the teeth of his zipper hissed. Maggie released the tab to reach inside his jeans. Her hand closed over the length of him, hard and hot through the thin cotton of his boxer briefs.

His fingers caressed her shoulders, easing under the straps of her green gown and sliding them from her shoulders until the bodice folded over, and her breasts spilled out. He palmed the weight of them, massaging them while he flicked his thumb across the distended nipples.

Maggie bit her lip, but her moan slipped out. She arched her neck, then her back, begging for more. He lowered his head. His hair brushed against her throat as he nuzzled her neck, shoulder, then slid his mouth lower. He nibbled at the curve of her breasts before closing his lips over a nipple and tugging.

Her legs weakened, and heat pooled between them. "Patrick!"

While one hand kept playing with her nipple, his other hand bunched her nightgown, lifting it up so that he moved his hand between her legs. As he pushed his fingers into her wetness, his breath shuddered out against her breast. "Oh, Maggie…sweet, sweet Maggie, I have to taste you…."

Boneless with desire, she leaned against him. He lifted her, but instead of carrying her, he settled her butt onto the hall table behind her, knickknacks and a bowl of potpourri clattering against the hardwood as he shoved them to the floor. He dropped to his knees in front of her, then lifted her legs so that they slid over his shoulders. His hands stroked over her inner thighs, making her shudder in anticipation and excitement. "Patrick…."

"You're so beautiful, Maggie," he murmured as his gaze traveled over her smooth thighs, flushed breasts, to meet her gaze. "So beautiful…."

Then he moved his mouth between her legs, bringing her such ecstasy that tears streaked from the corners of her eyes. "Oh, Patrick, more, more…"

He reached in his pocket for a condom packet that he tore open with his teeth, sheathing himself before rising up. With her legs still over his shoulders, he drove inside her.

Maggie shuddered and convulsed as an orgasm rippled through her. "Ohhhhh…" She moved her legs, locking them around his waist as he lifted her off the table. He shifted them, pushing her back against the wall as he drove into her, again and again.

Maggie stretched, taking him deeper than she'd ever taken anyone inside her. Her muscles clutched him tightly. He lowered his head, biting at her shoulder before nipping his way around the curve of her breasts. As his teeth closed over her nipple, she came again. Harder and hotter than she'd ever come before. She clawed at his shoulders and bit his neck, but still she couldn't hold in the scream burning her throat as the orgasm tore through her. "Patrick!"

He pumped harder, then stiffened. A guttural groan ripped from his throat as he came. His breath ragged gasps, he leaned his forehead against hers. "Maggie, you're going to kill me!"

"You're in great shape," she reminded him. "You can take it."

"Bed, I need a bed."

She gestured down the hall. He carried her, muscles rippling in his arms and shoulders. She'd left her door open, so he carried her through it. Scented candles filled the air with the sweet fragrance of cinnamon and vanilla.

"Did you know I was coming?" he asked as he gazed around the dimly lit room.

"I might have done this for me," she said as she slid from his arms.

"Oh, your other gift," he said, his voice deepening with a trace of jealousy as he referred to the vibrator.

"The last one."

"That wasn't the last gift, Maggie."

No, he was the last gift.

He reached into the pocket of his unzipped jeans. For another condom? Not only was he in great shape, he had amazing stamina. But when he pulled out his hand, a small metallic silver bag dangled from his finger.

A smile lifted her mouth. "I knew it was you."

"I wasn't exactly trying to keep it a secret," he admitted. "I wanted you to know it was me. I wanted you to know how much I wanted Maggie, the woman."

She'd figured that out. What she hadn't known until he'd started giving her the gifts was how much she'd wanted Maggie, the woman, too. "So this is the last gift?" she asked as she reached for the little bag; it was the smallest of the ones he'd given her.

He shook his head. "Oh, Maggie, I intend to give you many, many more…." His blue eyes gleamed in the candlelight, desire flashing as his gaze traveled up and down her body. He stepped closer and cupped her cheek with his free hand, gliding his thumb across her mouth, caressing her lower lip. "Here's your present. I'll be right back."

He walked through the open door of her master bath, leaving Maggie alone with the resurgence of desire heating her body. She turned her attention to the little bag he'd hooked around her finger, up-ending it over the flannel comforter. A key fell out, absorbing the candlelight so that it glowed. She hadn't expected a ring. Not yet. They weren't even really dating. But what was the key for? He hadn't bought her a car to replace her lemon, had he? Did he not want her calling the shop anymore?

Even though she'd kept his other presents, how could he think she would accept such an extravagant item? She prized her independence; surely, he knew that.

Warm lips slid across her throat, hands cupping her breasts as he came up behind her. His erection nudged against the small of her back.

"You shouldn't have, Patrick," she murmured, biting her lip as passion overtook her. Again. She'd never been so easily aroused. All he had to do was touch her…

He lifted her nightgown, parting her first with his fingers, then he slid deep inside her. Maggie bent over the bed, over the key, as he drove in again and again. His hands kneaded her breasts, her nipples squeezed between his fingers as he pounded into her.

She'd never known such raw need, such stark desire. Her breath shuddered out, then stopped as an orgasm crashed through her. Her heart hammered against her ribs, driven by passion and fear. How could he affect her so much, so deeply? He'd come to mean so much to her.

He withdrew, then drove deep. His body stiffened, his hands stilling. "Maggie!"

She melted onto the bed, body spent and throbbing with the aftermath of their lovemaking. She heard the water run after he stepped into the bathroom again. Then he was back, gathering her into his arms as he settled onto the bed with her.

"I shouldn't have done that?" he asked.

She couldn't control the smile that wearily lifted her lips. "No. That was…incredible…." Just when she thought it couldn't get any hotter between them…

She held up the key and tilted her face toward his. "You shouldn't have done this."

"Maggie, I know you don't have much free time, so I wanted you to know…any time you want me, you can come to me. It's a key to my house."

She drew in a ragged breath. God, that seemed so much more monumental than a car or an engagement ring. A key to his house.

"No pressure," he insisted.

She exhaled. "No pressure." And there wasn't. Patrick Mallehan was a strong man; he didn't want her in his life so she could take care of him. He didn't want to take care of her, either; he understood that she could do that herself. He only wanted her.

"I have something for you, too," she said.

"Cookies? Fudge?" he asked as he toyed with her hair, rubbing a strand between his fingers as if savoring the texture.

"No."

"Oh, Maggie," he said, sighing with disappointment, "you know I love my sweets."

"You might find something in the kitchen," she said. She'd made more chocolate-chip muffins, some cookies and fudge. But she didn't want to leave the bed, to leave his arms. Ever.

As if he'd read her mind, his arms tightened around her. "I'm happy right here."

"Me, too." Happier than she'd ever thought she could be. "But I do have a present for you."

"If it's under the tree, it'll have to wait," he said, his eyes closing.

"No, it's right here. I'm your present, Patrick Mallehan. For a week. Not only are the kids gone but Hal gave me the whole week off." Heat flushed her face at her presumptuousness. "I know you probably have to work, but—"

"Maggie, there's no place I'd rather be than with you." His throat moved as he swallowed, almost as if he choked on his next words. "But are you sure you want to spend your only free time with me? I know how busy you are, how much you're always doing for everyone else."

"I'm being selfish," she admitted. "Because your present is as much or more mine than yours. I want to be with you, Patrick." Her heart clenched as she realized she wanted more than a week with him.

"A week is good," he said, "but it's only the beginning. I want a lot more than a week with you, Maggie. If I hadn't thought it was too soon, I would have put a diamond in this last bag."

"It's not the last bag," she reminded him of his earlier promise.

"No, it's not." He kissed her forehead, tenderly, and his eyes glowed. He was falling for her just like she was falling for him. "I'm going to be in your life beyond this week, Maggie."

"Yes, you are."

While Brandon might struggle at first, hanging on to the dream of his parents reuniting just as he'd hung on to the idea of Santa Claus, her kids would eventually accept Patrick. They were smart kids; they'd realize what a good man he was. How good he was for their mother. Once she'd made time, it hadn't taken her long to realize how good he was for her.

With her secret Santa in her life, from now on every day would seem like Christmas. And Maggie O'Brien couldn't be happier.

* * * * *

YOU'RE ALL I WANT
FOR CHRISTMAS

SUSAN CROSBY

From the Author

Dear Reader,

Have you ever experienced a heart-stopping moment with a stranger? You know the one I mean—that old cliché about eyes meeting across a crowded room. Maybe your heart pounded a little louder. Maybe a small fantasy spun in your mind. And then reality stepped in, and the fantasy ended as you went your separate ways without even saying hello. Perhaps for a couple of days you thought about that searing connection and wondered...*what if?*

This is a story about two people who don't let that moment slip away. Lauren and Joe are stuck in an airport at Christmas, victims of the worst weather delay of the year. Their eyes meet. A small fantasy spins. They take the fantasy one step further....

Then *what if?* becomes *what now?*

I hope you enjoy Lauren and Joe's fantasy, a story about letting go of the past and living for the present, about how two people meant to be together find each other in an unlikely place. It's Christmas, after all, a magical time of year when the impossible becomes possible...if you wish hard enough.

Happy holidays.

Susan

For Lori Klarer, healer and friend.
You're a year-round gift.

CHAPTER 1

Sun, sand and margaritas...*that* was Lauren Wright's plan, her Christmas gift to herself. Instead, three days before Christmas, she'd gotten *this*— Chicago O'Hare Airport during the worst weather delays of the year.

Lauren glanced around the gate area, her home away from home the past two hours. Her gaze settled briefly on a man, one worthy of the second, third and tenth looks she'd given him. Mid-forties, she guessed, like her. Rugged, in a lumberjack sort of way. He wore jeans, a forest-green shirt and an aged brown leather jacket. Add to that his wavy chestnut hair, olive skin, and eyes so blue she could see the brilliant color from twenty feet away, and he was one tempting package.

But what also caught her attention was his patience—and the way he'd smiled at a couple of kids playing tag and teasing each other. Plus, in these days of laptop computers and cell phones seemingly permanently attached to bodies, he stood out for not being obsessively connected, just making an occasional cell phone call, probably checking in with someone.

"May I have your attention in the boarding area, please?" came a voice over the public address system. *"Flight 1529 to Phoenix is now ready for boarding."*

"The flight gods are with you," Lauren said to the woman seated next to her, who stood to gather her belongings.

"I may kiss the tarmac." The woman hefted her carry-on bag. "Good luck on yours."

"Thanks. I think maybe it's going to be a long day."

No sooner had the woman left than someone took her seat. A man. *The* man.

"I have a proposition for you," he said.

His eyes sparkled. His teeth flashed white. He smelled good. Really good. Like pine trees after a rainstorm.

Then his words registered. "A proposition?"

"I'll buy you a cup of coffee, if you'll save me this seat."

She felt her face heat up a little, her imagination having spun other much more interesting propositions. "I'd be happy to."

"Great, thanks. I'm Joe, by the way."

"Lauren."

"What would you like?"

You. Whoa. Where had that come from?

"What's your pleasure?" he asked as she remained silent.

"Pleasure?"

"Plain coffee? Designer?"

"Um. A decaf mocha would be good. No whipped cream."

"You got it."

He dropped his bag onto the chair and walked away, giving her the opportunity to really look at him—tall, sturdy, outdoorsy. Great butt.

Great everything.

And no wedding ring.

She pulled out a compact to check her hair and makeup, tucked her newly highlighted, shoulder-length hair behind her ears then added a fresh coat of Pomegranate Passion lipstick.

As good as it gets, she decided, returning her compact to her purse and eyeing his carry-on, a sturdy brown canvas bag, stuffed to the gills. Probably hadn't checked a suitcase, traveling light enough for just the one bag. Men could manage that better than women, especially women headed on vacation, who would need clothing and shoe options to survive the week.

"May I have your attention in the boarding area, please? Flight 265 to Salt Lake City has been delayed until 1:45."

Out of the corner of her eye she tracked Joe's return. She wished she'd kept her book out so that she could look occupied, but she'd given up on it an hour ago, since there was plenty to hold her attention in the overcrowded terminal, especially the man walking toward her, a mini-fantasy come to life.

He passed her the coffee, then took a seat.

"Thanks," she said, lifting it in a quick toast.

"My pleasure." He took out his cell phone and pushed one button, someone on his speed dial. "Hey. How's it going? Nope. It's been delayed again. One-forty-five, they're saying now…. I know, honey. Me, too."

Honey. So. Not wearing a wedding ring, but taken. The nice ones usually were.

"Call me whenever you want…. I wish I was there, too. Love you." He put away his phone then leaned back and took a sip.

"You must be headed to Salt Lake City," Lauren said. "I just heard the announcement."

"Yeah. Denver's weather sure screwed up the whole country, didn't it?" He nodded toward a kid who'd tossed his gear on the floor and crashed, falling asleep instantly and soundly. "So, what do you think his story is?"

"His story?"

"Where's he headed, do you suppose? Home from college for Christmas? Some happy mom waiting at the airport for him?"

She considered the young man, envying his ability to tune out the world and sleep in public. "A freshman." She cocked her head, considering. "Maybe not seeing his mom, yet. Maybe he's joining his father first to go skiing over Christmas, so now he's headed to Aspen to hook up with Dad and his new wife. Then he'll go home to spend the rest of his break with his mother—as much as a kid that age stays home," she added, smiling, remembering her first Christmas home as a freshman. She felt Joe's steady and sympathetic gaze on her, as if he knew it wasn't a story she was making up. "Just a guess," she added.

"First Christmas without your son?" Joe asked.

She nodded then sipped her mocha rather than add anything that might show how hurt she'd been by her son's choice. Jeremy could've gone skiing at New Year's instead, but he hadn't. Instead he'd chosen to leave her alone on Christmas—her worst day of the year.

Which was why she'd planned a getaway herself.

"Pretty ticked off at your ex for stealing him away?" Joe asked.

Had he been there and done that? "How'd you guess?"

He touched her hand for a second, the one holding—squeezing—the coffee cup. "I'm surprised you didn't pop the lid off."

Lauren went utterly still at the electrifying contact. The simple touch had zapped her clear down to her toes. Her eyes met his. She'd thought he'd sat beside her only so that he wouldn't lose a seat permanently, but maybe he'd been checking her out, too? Maybe even from a distance he—

"*May I have your attention in the boarding area, please? We regret to inform you that Flight 326 to Dallas-Fort Worth has been canceled. Please check with the customer service desk for assistance in making a new reservation.*"

Grumbling rippled through the area. Cell phones came out of pockets and purses. People gathered their possessions and moved away, other travelers immediately taking their places with grateful sighs at finding seats.

"That's an announcement I think we'll be hearing a lot," Joe said. "Where are you headed?"

"Nassau via Fort Lauderdale. My flight's still a go at this point, but there's an hour left. Who knows what'll happen by then?"

"Nassau? I wouldn't mind stretching out beside a pool, catching some rays."

"I left thirty-degree weather in Cedar Rapids this morning," she said, trying to dispel the image of him in swim trunks, a futile effort. She bet he looked spectacular. "I'd settle for anything above fifty."

"Same here, except I started in Portland, Maine."

"Really? My son goes to school at Bowdoin." The

college was only a short drive from Portland. "He's a biochem major and is on the Ultimate Frisbee team."

"You get to Portland often?"

"I haven't been allowed yet."

He grinned, which gave him extra appeal. A good sense of humor was high on her list of qualities she liked in a man. She thought she'd placed sex appeal a lot lower—until Joe had come within range, changing her mind, making her realize there really was such a thing as lust at first sight. She'd just never experienced it before.

He's taken, she reminded herself. *Taken.* Stop looking at him that way.

She decided she needed a break from him, needed to let her hormones settle down. "I think I'll go check on my flight," she said, standing. "Can I leave my suitcase here?"

"Of course. Lauren?"

"What?"

"I'm harmless."

Oh, no, you're not. "I have good instincts, Joe." And her instincts were shouting at her to be careful.

Lauren took her time. She checked her flight— now delayed an hour and set to leave about the same time as Joe's. She went to the restroom, then to buy something to snack on. She needed to relax; she couldn't believe that a little conversation and one small touch had affected her so much.

But nothing inside her relaxed, so she decided just to go with it, to enjoy the next hour or so as an adventure, and let herself be flattered by the way she occasionally caught him checking her out, and how content he seemed being near her. What could it hurt, after all? Ships passing in the night, that was all.

Having stalled long enough, she went back to her chair and told him about her delay as she opened the pack of peanuts and offered him some.

He shook out a few, then angled his head toward the left. "The couple dressed alike over there? What do you think?"

She'd noticed them before. "Married thirty years."

"Why do you say that?"

"They hardly talk. They've said it all."

"Or they're so comfortable with each other, they communicate a lot without words," he said.

She smiled at his whimsy. "There's a lovely thought. You're an optimist."

"No reason not to be. So, how long have you been divorced?"

"It's been final over a year." She didn't tell him how shaken her self-confidence had been or how slow the rebuilding of it. "He left the day after Christmas, two years ago."

"How sensitive."

His sarcasm made her smile. "His norm."

"So, good riddance?"

"Not at the time. But he married his reason for leaving, and I've recovered."

"As much as one recovers from such events."

"Are you speaking from experience?"

"I'm—" His cell rang. "Excuse me," he said, flipping the phone open. "Hey… No change so far. How about you? Yeah? What's the number there?" He pulled out a pen and wrote down a phone number on his ticket folder. "Are you allowed to use your cell? Okay, honey. You got it. Love you. It won't be long now."

He'd kept his voice upbeat, but Lauren saw something else in his eyes—sadness? Frustration? Fear? She didn't know him well enough to guess.

"My daughter, Anna," he said finally, tucking his phone in his pocket. "She's in labor with her first child. She and her husband are headed to the hospital now."

Honey was his daughter? "In Salt Lake City?"

"Yes." He poured out another handful of peanuts. "She called early this morning as soon as her contractions started. I was lucky enough to move my flight up two days, and delusional enough to think I might get there in time for the birth, since firsts often take a long time."

"You still may."

"Doubtful. But I'll see him or her within hours, I'm sure."

"You don't know about the sex?"

"I assume they had it." His eyes twinkled.

She smiled back. "Successfully, obviously."

"May I have your attention in the boarding area, please? We regret to inform you that Flight 143 to San Francisco has been canceled. Please proceed to the customer service desk for assistance in making a new reservation."

"Another one bites the dust. Things seem to be changing fast." Joe looked at his watch. "I should check on mine. What's your flight number? Might as well see about yours." He wrote it on his ticket folder. "Can I get you anything?"

"I'm fine, thanks."

Lauren saw several people coveting his vacated chair. She didn't blame them. It was hard waiting and wondering, but especially without having a place to sit comfortably. The restaurants had filled up, too, she'd noticed earlier, and the situation would only get worse as the day went on.

Lauren let her gaze wander without really seeing anything. The question of honey had been answered. And no mention of a wife, although his apparent understanding about Lauren's divorce seemed to indicate he'd been through one himself. It still didn't mean he wasn't attached.

She wondered if they lost their seats, would he still hang out with her?

What difference does it make? The words weren't whispering in her head but shouting, as if trying to tell her to get real. They would go their separate ways, would never see each other again.

So, why couldn't she just enjoy him for what he was—an extremely good-looking man who was interested enough in her to keep a conversation going. He could've buried his nose in a book, but he hadn't.

Get real, she reminded herself again. She was a reasonably attractive woman, yes, but she was also his age, and she knew from experience that most men over forty wanted women substantially younger. Her ex, for example. What he and Crystal talked about was anyone's guess....

Well, talking was probably low on their priorities.

"What are you smiling about?" Joe asked, sitting beside her again.

She didn't want to discuss her ex with this new and exciting man. "I'm wondering about the young couple across the way. The ones in jeans and sweat-shirts."

He contemplated them. "Sweethearts headed to her parents' house. Taking him home to introduce him to Mom and Dad. He's scared to death."

She shook her head. "They're not sweethearts."

"Okay, storyteller. What's your plot?"

"They just met today."

"What makes you say that?"

"The way they're flirting. She's twirling her hair. He's angled toward her, intent. It's brand-new. It'll be a story to tell their grandchildren—how they met at Chicago O'Hare during a weather delay and fell in love."

He watched them for a few seconds then turned his gaze on Lauren. "You think all relationships can be measured that way?"

"In body language? Yes, I do." She'd found herself leaning toward Joe as he talked, and had noted how he focused on her, as well. She liked the flattering looks he'd given her, making her feel good about herself. "It's universal, I think. Unless you're consciously making an effort to hide your reaction."

"I haven't noticed you twirling your hair."

Her cell phone rang, startling her, saving her from responding. She saw it was her sister Bobbie and didn't bother to say hello. "If you tell me it's a balmy seventy degrees, I'm hanging up."

"Would I do that to you? It's actually a balmy seventy-three."

"Not fair."

"I figure it's a bad sign that you've answered your phone."

"Hold on a sec." She tipped the phone down and asked Joe what he'd learned about their flights, realizing she'd been so intent on the body-language issue, she hadn't even asked.

"They're both delayed until further notice. No ETA. They're not even announcing them anymore, there are so many. I managed to flag down a customer service rep. She said that hundreds of flights have been canceled around the country, with probably hundreds more to come."

Lauren angled the phone up again. "Bobbie?"

"I heard. Who was that?"

"A fellow wayfarer. How's the hotel?"

"Everything the Web site said it was."

"Well, crap."

Bobbie laughed. "Yeah, a real shame that it's perfect. They have pool boys, Lauren. Gorgeous, studly pool boys. One just brought me a strawberry margarita."

"How's the competition?"

"Lots of couples roaming around. Haven't seen many singles, male or female, except for staff. But, heck, if there's a single man out there, I'd better stake my claim now, before *you* get here and become the competition. I'm ten years older than you."

"But young at heart."

"So, what about your fellow wayfarer? Cute?"

Lauren looked at Joe, who looked back, his brows raised. "Definitely cute."

He pointed to himself in question, and she nodded. He took it further by posing like a bodybuilder.

"And slightly deluded," she said to her sister with a laugh.

"Single?"

"Not sure." She looked at him. "Are you single?"

He raised his left hand. His ringless hand. Which didn't answer her question. Men.

"No ring," she said into the phone.

"Which means nothing, as you well know."

Lauren had to end the conversation, as Joe was enjoying the discussion way too much. No need to stroke his ego. He probably got plenty of strokes as it was. "I'll give you a buzz when I have news. About the flight," she added.

"I'll have a margarita for you. No, two. It'll be happy hour soon."

"Don't drive anywhere. Talk to you soon."

"You think I'm cute, huh?" Joe said as she slipped the phone back into her purse.

"So. We could be spending the night here?"

He grinned at her change of subject. "Looks like a possibility. At least we're not canceled yet. Means there's hope."

It was his turn for a cell phone interruption. "Hey! Where are you? They're at the hospital. Are you going straight there?"

Ex-wife? Lauren wondered, knowing that some

couples stayed friends after a divorce. She and her ex were civil to each other in public, but now that their son was on his own, she didn't often have a reason to communicate with his father. She hoped in time they could be friendly, especially when they eventually became grandparents to the same child.

"We're on undetermined delay. I doubt I'll make it…. Yeah, give her a kiss from me. Welcome the baby to the family…. Glad you could take off a couple days early and that your trip was smooth. Talk to you later."

Again Lauren noticed how his tone of voice didn't match his expression. Trying to stay upbeat took its toll.

"My son," he said.

Son. Not ex-wife.

"He's a junior at Arizona State. He drove to Salt Lake. Just got there."

"I gather you were both converging on your daughter's house for Christmas, anyway."

He nodded, absently stroking the phone with his thumb. "Christmas Eve was the plan."

It seemed like the perfect time to ask the most obvious question. "May I ask about their mother?"

CHAPTER 2

He looked into the distance, rubbing the empty place on his left ring finger. "Emily. She passed away last year."

"Oh, I'm so sorry." She laid a hand on his arm for a moment, finding it rigid with tension. When she started to pull back, he clasped her hand, keeping it there, then met her gaze.

"Thanks."

"I can't begin to imagine what you're going through."

He released her after a few seconds. "You talked about having recovered. So have I—except for times like this when something important is happening with one of the kids. Emily would've already been at Anna's house, in anticipation. I know Anna's missing her mom a whole lot right now."

Lauren's biggest regret in life was not having a daughter. Not that she would trade Jeremy for anything, but one child was all her body had been allowed, according to the doctors. Lauren had been so close to her own mother, had wanted that mother/daughter relationship for herself, but it wasn't meant to be. "Why does Anna live in Utah?"

"Her husband's job. They're high-school sweethearts. Met and married in Maine, and they would love to move back home, probably will soon. How about you? Having a hard time with your empty nest?"

"Yes and no. I've been preparing for Jeremy to leave home; you know, the next logical step for a child after high school. But I'd always expected I'd be part of a couple." She smiled and shrugged. "Best laid plans, hm?"

"It's all a crapshoot."

"How many times have you said that in your life?"

He laughed, low and soft. "Too many to count."

"Me, too. It's pretty much my motto, even though the engineer in me doesn't like anything that isn't logical. I prefer to determine my own destiny."

"You're an engineer?" he asked, angling toward her more.

"Technically I'm a drafting technician, but I'm also an engineer-in-training. I take someone's design and turn it into a blueprint. But my goal is to become a designer. Not an architect, mind you, but the person who works with the builder to actually *create* the design and, subsequently, the blueprint. I've even had the opportunity to work directly with a builder twice in the past couple of months. I loved it. It's my calling. How about you?"

His grin was crooked. "I'm a builder."

Her heart leaped into her throat. "You're serious?"

"Thirty years, third-generation."

"So...we speak the same language."

"Isn't it romantic?"

Lauren laughed. She was good at her job because she was meticulous to a fault, and also logical. Too logical. Not romantic at all. It was one of the things that ruined her marriage, according to her ex. In marriage and in life, she didn't see the big picture as much as the details. She could chew on details forever, was overly cautious.

And builders were notorious risk-takers, ending up with big rewards or huge crashes. She'd always figured she'd be a good balance for someone like that.

"There's a crowd gathering over there," Joe said. "I'll go check it out. Be right back. Can I get you anything?"

"I'm good."

Widowed. Lauren tried to imagine that kind of pain, so entirely different from a divorce. So...final.

But, recovered? How could he be? Like everyone else, she'd heard there was a magic one-year mark when one was supposed to be healed, when it was okay to start dating, when mourning ended. Officially, perhaps, but truly? Emotionally? She didn't see how.

Keeping watch for him, she called her sister.

"On your way?" Bobbie asked immediately.

"No news. I need an answer quick, okay? After John died, how long did it take you to recover? I mean really recover, beyond just wanting to date. You know, wanting to make a real connection with someone. I can't remember what your timeline was."

"Does this have anything to do with your fellow wayfarer?"

"Yes," she hissed. "I need an answer right now, Bobbie."

"Two, maybe closer to three years. But everyone recovers at their own pace, Lauren. And men react differently, too. Are you saying you're getting serious about this man? A total stranger?"

"I don't want to. He's just so…appealing."

"How long has he been widowed?"

"At least a year. I don't know specifically."

There was a long pause, then, "Just be careful, okay?"

"Because?"

"I think you're both in very tender places right now. I know *you* are."

"Tender? What do you— Shoot. He's coming back. I'll call you later." She pressed End and dropped the phone in her purse.

"Just an airline rep trying to soothe nerves," he said, sitting beside her.

"May I have your attention in the terminal, please?

The following flights have been canceled for today. Please proceed to the customer service desk to make new reservations."

Lauren listened for her flight, but it wasn't called. Nor was Joe's.

"Some new form of torture," she said to him. "See how long until we lose our cool."

"Or our minds. I'm not sure whether this means we can hope. Every time in the past I've been involved in a weather delay, I eventually made it out the same day."

Around them, passengers reacted to the news, some heading out immediately, others realizing that making a cell phone call to the airline would result in faster service. Chairs filled up as fast as they were emptied.

An elderly couple made their way into the seating area. Lauren touched Joe's arm and nodded toward the couple.

"I'm pretty sick of sitting here," she said.

"You took the words out of my mouth."

They gestured to the couple, offering their seats, then grabbed their bags and moved away.

"Married sixty years," Joe said as they walked. "Still deeply in love."

"Never gave up, even during the toughest times," Lauren added. "Came close once, but stuck it out and came back even stronger."

"Now who's the optimist?" He smiled.

"You're obviously contagious."

Lauren waited to see what the change of venue would do to their situation. They would no longer have to save seats for each other, since floor space was available in pockets all around the terminal. Would he go it alone now?

"That looks like a good spot," he said, pointing. "Want to put down stakes?"

She started to say sure, then stopped. She was in way over her head here. She knew what would happen. They would talk some more and share some confidences. She would feel sympathy for him, start to feel proprietary. Then they would board their flights, go their separate ways, and she would spin fantasies about him for weeks about what could've been, driving herself crazy.

Did she really want to put herself through that?

Bobbie's words echoed— *Be careful.* And her own words to herself— *Get real.*

"I think I'll go wander for a while," she said to Joe finally.

"Okay."

"It was nice talking to you."

Surprise registered on his face. "You can leave your bag. I won't go anywhere until you come back. Or I can come with you."

"I appreciate the offer. I think I'd just like some time alone."

"That sounds…final, Lauren."

"No, I—" Really, what could she say? "I just don't want you to feel tied down with my suitcase."

He hesitated. "Okay."

She walked away, but she hadn't gone fifty feet before she regretted it. She kept going, although much more slowly, chastising herself. *Lauren Wright, you are such an idiot. He's good company. Why are you trying to be alone when he's offering companionship? You have someone to talk to. Why are you throwing that away?*

She turned back, saw he'd given in to a need to sleep, stretching out on the floor like one of the teenagers, resting against his carry-on. It looked as if his eyes were closed.

She decided to let him sleep. Every so often she checked their flights. Theirs didn't change but many more cancellations were popping up, one rare departure. Public-address announcements had stopped almost entirely. People formed impatient lines at the gates, badgering the employees, tempers getting shorter and shorter.

She saw Joe jerk awake and pull out his cell phone to answer. After a couple of minutes he put it away then dragged a hand down his face. Bad news? Oh, she hoped not.

Lauren couldn't stand not knowing. She headed back and sat on the floor beside him.

"Am I still welcome?" she asked.

"Of course. Feeling better?"

What could she say? *I spent the past hour just watching you sleep*. It was the most adolescent thing she'd done since…she'd been an adolescent. "Yes, thanks. How about you?"

"Stiff." He rolled his shoulders. "My son just called. The contractions have stalled."

"Is that good? I mean, I know that means you still might make it in time, but does it also mean it's false labor or something?"

"They're not sure. They're monitoring closely, in case they need to take quick action."

"This is hell on you," she said softly, touching the back of his hand, wishing she could hug him.

"Yeah." The word dragged along his throat. He captured her hand and held tight. "I'm glad you're here. I needed someone to talk to."

"And you can't let on to your children how scared you are now."

He shrugged, a masculine form of agreement.

"Did you get to see your children be born?" she asked.

He managed a smile, then seemed to realize he was squeezing the feeling out of her hand and let go. "Most amazing and frightening experiences of my life."

A furious passenger started making a lot of noise

at the gate nearest them. He wasn't saying anything that everyone else in the terminal wasn't saying or thinking, but he was saying it much louder and more profanely.

"Just tell us the truth. That's all we want!" the man yelled. It escalated into a shouting match with the gate attendants before a couple of security guards intervened to restrain him, then a man in a suit spoke quietly and calmly to him, and escorted him away.

"Where do you suppose they're taking him?" Lauren asked.

"Probably arranged for a first-class flight tomorrow and are sending him to a hotel, on them."

She smiled. "Well, there's a fantasy. Do you think if I go make a big fuss, I might get to spend the night at the Four Seasons?"

"The fact that you call it a 'fuss' says everything about you."

"In what way?"

"That you probably don't know how to have a shouting match."

"Do you?"

"I used to. I take things a lot easier now."

"Because of Emily?"

"Partly. But maturity also reared its ugly head at some point. I didn't want my children to think yelling was the best approach to dealing with problems." He slid a hand over his stomach. "I don't know about you, but I'm hungry. How about I buy you dinner?"

Lauren had a vision of her sinking deeper and deeper in his quicksand of temptation then being left without a way to pull herself out. She remained silent long enough that he leaned toward her and said quietly, "Do you ever just go with your gut?"

"What do you mean?"

"It's only dinner."

She really was being extraordinarily protective of herself. Why was that? Because he was different? Because her pulse drummed a hard, fast cadence around him? Because she had yearnings she hadn't felt in a very long time just looking into those gorgeous blue eyes? Because he was not just a decent man, but an exciting one? Yes to all of those questions. If they had more time, she could fall in—

"Okay," she said in a rush, standing. She didn't want to let in the thoughts that had been about to invade her mind like Attila the Hun on a quest. What was she, crazy? She'd just met Joe. "Dinner would be great. Do you think we can get a table anywhere?"

"Let's go find out."

They automatically stopped in front of the airline monitors.

"Canceled," she said after a moment of shock.

He met her stunned gaze. "Mine, too."

CHAPTER 3

He offered his phone. "I've got the airline on speed dial."

"It's more important that you get your flight ASAP." She found the airline's number in her phone's memory.

It took Lauren exactly thirty-four patience-trying minutes to rearrange her flights, including being put on hold twice. Joe was done sooner and then made other calls.

"Tomorrow morning, ten-fifteen," she said to him when she hung up.

"Tomorrow afternoon, three-ten." He couldn't hide his frustration.

"Oh, no. That's the earliest flight they have?"

"The earliest with space available."

"Can you go on standby before that one?"

"Apparently my chances are nil."

"Your daughter must be very upset."

He nodded. His jaw flexed.

She decided he didn't want to talk about it anymore. "I need to call my sister and tell her about the change."

"That's who you were talking to earlier?"

"Yes. We are two of four sisters. Bobbie's the oldest and I'm the youngest." She dialed. "She's been widowed for five years— Guess what?" she said when Bobbie answered.

"You've been canceled."

"How'd you know?"

"A fellow wayfarer here has a laptop and Wi-Fi. He's been checking on your flight for me."

"A fellow wayfarer, huh?" She looked at Joe and smiled. "Is he cute?"

"He's sixteen and bored out of his skull. His parents dragged him on vacation, away from his girl-friend, but he's got gizmos and gadgets to keep him connected with everyone and everything in the time-space continuum. And to answer your question, yes, he's cute, although a little too intense for me."

Lauren laughed. "Not to mention young."

"That, too. So, what happens now?"

She told Bobbie about the new reservations.

"Where will you stay tonight?"

The magic question. "I'm not sure. I've been hear-ing snatches of conversations about how all the hotels near the airport are full. I'm not crazy about the thought of camping out at O'Hare."

"Why would you do that? You've got plenty of time to go into the city and enjoy an evening in that toddlin' town. It's only around four o'clock there, right? Chicago's weather isn't causing the problems. You're not snowed in at O'Hare."

"Right." Like she'd go out on the town alone. Sure. "I'll let you know when I've settled someplace." She closed the phone and met Joe's waiting gaze. "So."

He smiled. "Indeed."

"What are you going to do?"

"I just made a reservation at a hotel in the city."

Disappointment landed on her like a lead blanket. She had her answer. He'd just been killing time with her. She stuck out her hand. "I enjoyed talking with you, Joe. Best of luck to you and your daughter."

He ignored her outstretched hand for a long moment, then took it and moved a step closer. "I made you a reservation, too, which you're welcome to use or cancel, but I figured the good places might fill up fast."

"Oh. I—"

"Before you retreat to think it over," he interrupted with a slight smile, "let me say this. I'd like to spend the evening with you. I'd like to take you someplace nice for dinner and continue our conversation. Please don't read more into it than that." He stopped, closed his eyes for a second, then said, "That's a lie, frankly. I find you attractive, Lauren.

Very attractive. So, you can read that into it. But I'm a man of my word, and my word is that I will treat you with respect."

But will I do the same? Lauren wondered. *Oh, for heaven's sake. He finds you attractive. What is your problem?*

"I need to know something first," she said.

"Shoot."

"Are you seeing someone?"

"No."

Lauren found that astonishing, given his obvious qualities.

"You don't believe me," he said, letting go of her hand, pulling back.

She'd obviously struck a nerve, as if she'd questioned his integrity. "It's not that," she said instantly. "I'm just amazed."

"So am I—about you. You *are* uninvolved, right?"

She hadn't looked at it that way. Lauren didn't consider herself exceptional. "I'm uninvolved."

"Then let's just start over," he said, extending his hand. "Hi, I'm Joe—"

She put a hand over his mouth. "No last names."

He frowned. "Why not? I want you to know that I'm on the up-and-up. That you can trust me."

"If I didn't already trust you, I wouldn't be saying yes to your invitation."

"It's a two-way street, you know. I also trust you."

"Yes, but we both also know this is a fantasy, Joe. Let's not try to make it real. It's an evening. One evening."

He smiled as if humoring her. "If those are the rules, I'll play by them. Anything to spend more time with you."

"Flattery will get you everywhere."

"Yeah? Okay, your eyes are like semisweet chocolate chips, your lips like maraschino cherries, your hair like honey dripping over peanut butter—"

"You *are* hungry."

For just a few moments his gaze heated up. Her pulse thudded loud in her ears. Arousal flowed through her, warm and heavy.

"Not just hungry. Starving," he said.

"Me, too." Was this how the night was going to go? Each of them saying things with double meanings? Each of them looking at the other with desire?

"The night awaits, Lauren."

The night awaits. She liked the sound of that—an exciting unknown.

They fell into step beside each other, not talking, occasionally glancing at each other as they made their way through the terminal. Outside, winter assaulted them, the windchill taking the temperature lower than what they'd each left behind that morning.

In the cab, neither of them hugged the doors but each sat more toward the center of the backseat, so that their arms grazed during turns. Their chatty driver answered questions and pointed out landmarks during the forty-five-minute trip.

Internally Lauren crackled with anticipation. What would the evening hold? She usually liked everything planned out, but had let that need go, along with her last name, as a way of keeping the fantasy alive.

He seemed on edge, too, but maybe it had more to do with his daughter giving birth. Every time he talked to her or his son, he would take Lauren's hand and squeeze it.

The cab eased into a hotel driveway. Lauren spotted an elegant sign: Four Seasons Hotel Chicago.

She fired a look at Joe, who looked pleased that he'd surprised her, having picked up on her comment at the airport and reserving rooms at one of the classiest, priciest hotels in town. Could she afford to stay there?

Can you afford not to? It's only money, after all….

"You don't have to keep the reservation," he said quietly as a uniformed man approached the car. "But this way you're guaranteed something. And it's connected to The 900 Shops, so we could entertain ourselves for the evening without going out into the weather."

Lauren could think of other ways for them to entertain themselves….

"I see you need to think it over," he said, his eyes laughing at her predictability. "Let's store our luggage and go have dinner. That should give you enough time."

Oh, she wanted to kiss that smiling mouth and see how he tasted and felt. She hadn't been drawn to anyone so much, so quickly, in such a long time, maybe since her courtship days more than twenty years ago. Maybe. She couldn't remember exactly how she'd felt then.

Lauren thanked him, appreciating his sensitivity, as her door was opened and a man welcomed them to the Four Seasons.

"Checking in?" he asked.

"Yes," Joe answered. "But we'd like to store the luggage while we go eat first. We've been stuck at O'Hare all day."

Lauren moved out of the way, not wanting to hear Joe's last name, which he would certainly have to give the bellman in order to have their bags held. The fanciful thought of keeping their last names from each other seemed a little silly now that she'd had time to think about it. Why not know his name? Why not let him know hers?

But she didn't want to regret the decision, either. There would be plenty of time to share names, if she changed her mind.

"The hotel has a couple of restaurants," Joe said when he came up beside her. "Very nice ones, as you can imagine. But there's also a Johnny Rockets in the mall, which the valet says has great hamburgers."

"I'm for whatever is fastest. A burger sounds great."

Without their carry-on bags they could make their way much faster, and they were seated and dinner was ordered before much time passed.

Joe set his cell phone on the table.

"Why don't you just call?" Lauren asked, seeing concern in his eyes. He hadn't heard anything for at least an hour.

"Because they'll say, 'You know, Dad, we *will* call when there's something to tell you.'"

"I think they would forgive a protective father."

"I'll wait a little while longer."

She spun her water glass slowly, catching the drops of condensation with her fingertips. "How do you feel about becoming a grandpa?"

"Old."

She laughed.

"My grandfathers were gray-haired and wore cardigans," he said. "I don't want to picture myself like that."

"How old are you?"

"Forty-eight."

Three years older than she. "And how old were they when you were born?"

"Younger," he said after a minute, as if stunned at the realization.

They continued a casual conversation then dug into their food, demolishing it as if they'd been stuck on a deserted island for days instead of in an airport for hours, where food had been available. When their mouths weren't stuffed, they spoke about favorite restaurants and best-ever vacations, nothing personal.

Lauren wished she could say she'd relaxed, but the truth was, she got more wound up by the minute. She hadn't wanted to like him so much and almost wore herself out looking for red flags and fatal flaws.

When the conversation switched to music, he told her he liked jazz.

"Jazz makes me nervous," she said. "There's no order to it."

"Which is what I like about it. My life has enough order."

It was a telling statement, one of the most revealing about himself so far, she thought. He didn't like to be boxed in.

"What do you listen to?" he asked as their server brought his credit card and receipt back to him.

"Country, mostly."

"Makes sense for you, I think. Country songs tell a story. You'd like the logic of that."

She didn't want him to think she was all logic and no fun. She could be fun and spontaneous. She was sure of it. She just needed the opportunity....

They left the restaurant then stopped outside the entrance. A decision awaited them, one of a string of decisions they'd made all day, leading to this point.

"Do you want to check in now?" he asked. When she didn't answer instantly, he added, "Before you tell me, I think you should know something. I've been having a helluva time keeping my hands off you, but I have and will continue to. The difference between us, I think, is that you're fighting the attraction while I've accepted it. It doesn't mean I'm less attracted than you. It means my parents raised me to be civilized." He leaned a little closer. "Even though I'm not feeling entirely civilized at the moment. You do something to me that I can't even describe."

Lauren's body temperature spiked at his words. No one had wanted her that much. No one. So, how much was a fantasy worth?

Plenty. Certainly the price of a room at the Four Seasons.

"I'll stay. Thank you, Joe."

He nodded.

"I wouldn't mind wandering through the shops for a while, however," she said. She'd avoided the malls at home, steering clear of Christmas in general, as she had the year before, except for shopping for Jeremy and decorating the house a little because she had to. If she hadn't, Jeremy would've questioned her about it, since it used to be her favorite holiday and she normally went all out decorating and baking and shopping. Her ex had ruined that by leaving her the day after Christmas, turning her favorite holiday into something she dreaded instead.

But her bigger reason for not checking in to the hotel yet was that she didn't want the evening to end—or even be interrupted.

"Anything in particular you'd like to shop for?" he asked.

"Well, I'm sure the hotel will provide a robe, but I need something to wear to bed."

Her words danced in the air like Fourth of July starbursts, bright and loud.

Heat shimmered in his eyes. "I hate to ask the obvious, but…"

"But what?"

"Why do you need to wear anything at all?"

CHAPTER 4

Lauren had never slept naked. Never. Ever. And in a hotel? No way. What if there was a fire or some other catastrophe and she had to run into the hallway? She would buy a long T-shirt or nightshirt, something practical that she could wear at home.

"Never mind," he said, smiling at her discomfort.

They hadn't taken ten steps before his cell phone rang. He hesitated just long enough that she saw panic in his eyes. His hands shook as he put the phone to one ear and pressed his fingers to the other, blocking the Christmas music and crowd noise. He ducked his head, as if it would help.

Lauren took his arm and pulled him into a nearby shop, wondering why he wasn't saying anything, worried that something had gone wrong.

He stayed hunched, listening intently, then finally he smiled, tentatively at first, then broadly, happily. He angled the phone so that Lauren could hear, too. A baby cried, that distinctive newborn sound that always made parents take deep breaths of relief and almost collapse with indescribable happiness.

"It's a girl, Dad," she heard a woman say from a distance. "Say hello to Mariah Emily. Joey's got the phone to her ear."

"Welcome to the world, Mariah Emily," Joe said, his voice raspy. "This is your grandpa, and I already love you."

Tears sprang to Lauren's eyes as he put the phone back up to his ear and talked to his daughter in a tender voice that tugged at Lauren's heart. She wandered away, letting him speak in private. She finally noticed the shop she'd pulled him into—an electronic-games store filled mostly with teenage boys, oblivious to the small drama being played out in front of them.

She saw Joe slide his phone into his pocket then drag a hand down his face, a gesture she would always associate with him. She waited for him to indicate he was ready for company again. Finally he looked up, and his expression was almost too much to bear—relief, joy, disappointment came spilling from him in quick succession.

She moved toward him. As soon as she was within arm's reach, he grabbed her and pulled her close, wrapping his arms around her, clinging to her.

Lauren hugged him back, hard. She couldn't say anything that wouldn't seem like a cliché, so she said nothing, just rubbed his back and let him hold on.

She didn't know how long they stood there, but he finally released her, slowly, reluctantly, it seemed. She put her hands on his face.

"Congratulations, Gramps."

He smiled then kissed her palm. The smile left his face by degrees as they stared at each other. She let her hands drift to his shoulders then along his arms. After a moment he leaned down and kissed her, a soft brush of contact. He groaned quietly. She dug her fingers into his forearms, so hard and capable. He moved closer—

A wolf whistle pierced the air—one of the teenagers reminding them of their very public location.

They moved into the mall again and walked without talking. He reached for her hand. She automatically pulled away, then a few seconds later, settled her hand in his. She finally registered his calluses, proof of hard, physical work. She liked how his skin felt against hers.

Stars filled Lauren's world, inside and out. Suddenly she was aware of Christmas in a way she hadn't been until this moment, even though they'd been surrounded, engulfed really, by the season, with endless carols coming from the mall-wide sound system and decorations everywhere. She found herself humming. Elation surged through her. She was happy to be alive, to be stuck by weather delays, to have met Joe, to have been there when he got the news of his granddaughter's birth. And she was happy to be walking through the mall, hand in hand, forgetting the memories she'd been running from when she planned her trip.

"Where to?" Joe asked.

"I think you should come bearing gifts for your granddaughter. How about Bloomingdale's? We can pick out something dainty."

"And you still need a nightgown."

She caught his gaze. "Yes. I wonder what time the store closes."

As soon as they got inside, they asked a clerk that question—only a half hour until closing.

They raced through the store to the infants' department, found a gorgeous white baby dress with matching cap and booties, totally impractical but perfect for her first professional photograph. Then they rushed to lingerie.

"Choose well," he said softly, intimately. He tucked her hair behind her ear then rubbed her earlobe for just a moment. "I'll meet you out front."

She started to tell him he could stay—what did it matter if he saw the flannel nightshirt she would buy—then decided even that was too intimate.

She watched him walk away, her ear tingling. Choose well? What did that mean? Choose something to entice him? And why was she hesitating?

Fear of rejection? Lack of self-confidence? Both those things perhaps, to a degree, but mostly the belief that they couldn't have more than one night. They lived too far apart to develop a relationship beyond the fantasy. And she wasn't a one-night-stand kind of woman. At least, she never had been.

Bobbie was right, too. They were in tender places and vulnerable, for entirely different reasons. It wasn't the right time to be indulging in fantasies that would be hard to recover from.

Or would those fantasies help in the long run? Turn an ordinary existence into something a little extraordinary?

Lauren stood amid the clothing racks, trying to make up her mind about what to buy. She fingered a snowman-printed flannel nightshirt. Warm, practical…

She made her purchase then caught up with him. He was leaning against the wall just outside the doors, not looking like anyone's grandfather. A couple of women gave him the eye but he didn't even notice.

Was he missing Emily? Of course he was. Their first grandchild had just been born. They should be celebrating, toasting the occasion, and going to bed wrapped in each other's arms to talk about the past and present and future.

Joe pushed away from the wall as she approached, his expression welcoming.

"Happy with what you got?" he asked, mischief in his eyes.

She slipped her arm through his, the boldest thing she'd done since she'd met him. "Happy in general. Thank you so much for this. All of this."

"Not exactly a hardship for me, Lauren." His phone rang, startling both of them. "Hi, honey. How's it going? Is she? I'm glad…. I'll bet Craig's on cloud nine…. Yes, I do remember. You were red and wrinkled and *loud*." He laughed at whatever she said. "No, you were pink and soft and I fell madly in love at first sight."

Lauren started to pull away, but he put his arm around her shoulders and kept her close.

"I'm fine, Anna. Of course, I'm disappointed not to have been there, but, you know, sometimes life throws a curve at you and you just have to go with it. You get some sleep now, okay? Let everyone pamper you. I'll talk to you in the morning…. Love you, too, honey. G'night."

"We need champagne," Lauren said as he put his phone away.

"I agree. Shall we go to the hotel bar?"

"Sounds good."

"Do you want to check in first?"

He hadn't come out and asked her to sleep with him. Would he? Or was he waiting for her to bring it up? Was part of checking in making the decision to share one room?

"Let's just go celebrate first," she said, still putting

off any decisions, which was probably not a good idea, since she would then be making decisions while under the influence.

They strolled through the mall toward the hotel. Santa was holding court in his big chair with his last customer, a little girl about five years old who sat on his lap talking seriously and endlessly, her blond curls bouncing.

"Jeremy hated Santa," Lauren said.

"I didn't know any child *could* hate Santa."

"Maybe *hate* is the wrong word. He was afraid of him. The idea of this big man wearing all red and having that long white hair and beard turned Jeremy into a nervous wreck. We had to avoid the Santas at the malls. We never watched a Christmas special with Santa in it."

"Poor little guy. What about presents?"

"We just had to tell him from very early on that Santa wasn't real, and we never gave him presents from Santa. Made for some tricky moments with his believer friends."

The little girl on Santa's lap continued to talk, as Santa nodded and nodded and nodded. The parents waited, adoring looks on their faces, while two of Santa's helpers rolled their eyes at each other, probably more because they wanted to go home.

"I loved being a mom," she said wistfully as she and Joe started walking again. "I loved everything about it. He always had a bunch of friends hanging out. I think that also made the adjustment to his going away to college hard. It wasn't just Jeremy leaving home, but the noise and fun of all his friends being around, too."

"Aside from your job, how do you fill your time?"

"Five friends and I started a cooking club. We meet once a month to make dinner, something exotic and challenging. I go to a lot of live theater productions. I read. And garden. How about you?"

They stepped into the hotel elevator and climbed to the seventh floor.

"I work."

"That's all?"

"Eat, sleep, work. That's about it."

"Do you date?" Her timing was all wrong for asking the question. She'd spoken just as they exited the elevator and hunted for the bar, so she couldn't tell whether he was delaying answering until they were in the bar or was going to ignore the question altogether, but he lifted a brow at her question.

They were seated in a dark-wood-paneled room, the lighting soft, making the elegant space feel cozy.

Joe ordered champagne, then he set his fists on the table and leaned toward Lauren. "Let's make a rule."

She could guess. "No personal questions."

"On the contrary, I think we should ask anything

we want. That doesn't mean we have to answer, but that it's okay to ask, to wonder. I'm curious, too, you know."

"About what?"

He opened his arms in a broad gesture. "Everything. You fascinate me."

"I do?"

"Yeah."

Since she was pretty certain she hadn't fascinated anyone else, she wasn't sure what to make of that comment.

"Is the rule okay with you?" he asked.

"Sure."

"Okay. So, in answer to your question, yes, I have dated. Twice."

"Two different women or the same woman twice?"

"Two different women, once."

"How old were they?"

He sat back, looking perplexed. "I never asked. Younger."

"By a lot?"

"Depends on your definition. They were both in their thirties."

"Early or late?"

He laughed finally. "You're like a dog with a bone about this subject. Why?"

"I'm testing a theory I have."

"I take it your ex is with someone much younger."

"Seventeen years."

He whistled, low. "Hard on the ego?"

"Not so much anymore, but it was in the beginning."

Their server delivered two flutes of champagne. She lifted her glass toward Joe. "To the first of your next generation. May her life be filled with wonder."

They clinked glasses then sipped, staring at each other all the while.

"How about you?" he asked. "You've dated, I assume."

"Six and two halves."

"Two halves?"

"I showed up for my half, but they didn't."

"You got lucky."

She smiled. "Yeah. It's good to find out if someone's a jerk early on. Saved me a lot of grief."

"And the men you date tend to be older?"

"Mostly."

"So, you've come to the conclusion that we're all looking for a young woman as an ego boost or something?"

"In my experience."

"You're a beautiful woman, Lauren, no matter what your age."

"I wasn't looking for compliments." *Liar.* "And I'm forty-five."

"Ah, good. A younger woman, then. I'm relieved.

I couldn't have gone on otherwise." His eyes sparkled.

"I guess my theory sounds pretty lame," she said, taking a sip, enjoying the bubbles and tangy flavor of the champagne.

"It sounds like the voice of experience."

"But it's not a fair representation of your entire gender."

"I hope not," he said, his tone light. "What makes you happy, Lauren?"

"My son. My work. The sun coming up. I love to watch the sun rise. How about you?"

"Breathing."

She laughed, but she knew what he meant.

"And being here with you," he added, much more seriously. He reached across the table and took her hand. "I don't want the evening to end."

Her breath caught in her throat. "I don't, either."

He rubbed his thumb over her tingling skin. "Here's what I propose. We cancel our two room reservations and get one suite, so we can continue our conversation as long as we want. You can have the bedroom, and I'll take the sofa. I'm sure the bedroom door locks."

"Would that be to keep you safe from me?" she asked, making a nervous joke.

He didn't smile. "You need to feel safe. I understand that. Even if the door doesn't lock, you don't need to worry." Then he sat back. One side of his mouth tipped up. "I figure you need to think about it, so don't answer yet."

"You've gotten to know me pretty well."

"As I said, you fascinate me."

She didn't get tired of hearing that.

"One last thing," he said. "If you have questions about Emily, ask them now. Because if we do share a suite tonight, I want it to be about us, okay? Not about Emily or—I don't even know your ex's name."

"Henry."

"Okay. Rule number two, then—after we leave the bar, Emily and Henry disappear. So, do you have any questions about her, or would you rather not know?"

She wasn't sure how much she wanted to learn about his late wife, but thought that what he told her on his own would probably answer more questions than her asking them. "Why don't you just give me a synopsis?"

He stared into his glass for a few seconds first. "It's not an extraordinary story. We married at twenty-two, and we had a good partnership, with the same ups and downs as everyone else. Most of the time we meshed. Sometimes we were out of sync. But we loved each other, and that never changed. We both grew a lot, changed a lot. She got ovarian cancer about five years ago, fought it, and thought she'd beaten it, but a couple of years later it came back and spread. Everywhere. That time she lost the battle."

Lauren could tell by the speed and force of his voice how much emotion drove his words. He needed to just get it out. "You miss her."

He didn't answer right away. "I have adjusted to life without her, and her last couple of years were a slow, tragic deathwatch. I don't miss her in the day-to-day way I did in the beginning. And I remember the good times, sure, but I haven't put her on a pedestal either. She was the biggest part of my life, and I've had to find myself anew since then, and without my children, who had already moved away from home. But I'm at peace with my life."

Lauren could see that he believed that, that he felt ready to move forward.

"Em and I had a lot of discussions, as you can imagine, about what I would do. She didn't want me to mourn for long. One of the things I'm doing is building a new home, a summer place on a little lake near the New Hampshire border. I've had the property for years, traded it for some work I did. I needed something that was mine, something to acknowledge the new phase in my life." He swigged his champagne, draining the glass. "That about sums it up."

"Thank you for sharing that."

"Your turn."

"Is there something you want to know? Because I don't feel any strong need to talk about him."

"I take it the divorce was a surprise to you."

"Complete and utter. I had no suspicion whatsoever that he was unhappy or cheating. I felt so stupid for not seeing it. But, like you, I've adjusted. Most of the time, I'm just fine with everything."

"Most of the time."

"I don't miss *him* so much as just being part of a couple. We are a paired-up world."

"How did your son react to the divorce?"

She remembered the hurt and the fury Jeremy had hurled at Henry. "He didn't speak to his father for months, which is why I didn't say anything when he made the decision to go to Aspen with his father. They've hardly spent any time together for almost two years. I hope they mend their relationship."

"And the dates that you went on, did you have fun?"

"I did, mostly. Two of the relationships lasted a couple of months each and ended okay. Anything in particular you want to ask?"

"Yeah. If Henry came to you and said he'd made the biggest mistake of his life, what would you do?"

"Wow. You don't pull any punches, do you?"

"We don't have time for that."

She pushed her empty glass away. "I wouldn't want him back."

"Not even for Jeremy's sake?"

"Not even. Too much was said and done. Any other questions?"

"Just one." He locked his gaze with hers. "Have you decided?"

She didn't hesitate this time. "Yes."

CHAPTER 5

The forty-fourth-floor suite overlooked downtown Chicago; the view of the city was breathtaking. The room's European-design decor soothed, the colors were rich and inviting, transporting Joe and Lauren to another world. A king-size bed dominated the bedroom like a leap of faith, the double-bed sofa in the living room its safety net. Two bathrooms allowed for individual privacy. In the living room, an entertainment system, dining table and wet bar completed the communal area.

It was way too much—too much space, too expensive, too unlike how Lauren perceived her Holiday Inn self, down to earth and practical.

But she loved it. The luxury made her feel that she mattered, that she was of value to Joe. He wouldn't let her pay for half of it, and she didn't want to examine too closely why she'd let him splurge on her.

There would be time for thinking later. Much later. Tonight was about fantasies—creating and fulfilling them. It was about Joe and Lauren, no one else.

And it *would* only be for one night. She wouldn't—couldn't—think beyond that.

Lauren glanced around the marble bathroom as she dried her hands, enjoying a few minutes alone for the first time all day. What she wanted was a long soak in the sumptuous tub, but she thought it might send the wrong signals if she came out all damp and warm, as if she expected to make love, when in fact she didn't know if they would even sleep, much less sleep together. Those issues would find their own resolutions at some point.

She left her sweater and shoes in the bedroom, unbuttoned one more button on her silk blouse to show a hint of cleavage, then padded barefoot into the living room. Unobtrusive background music filtered through multiple speakers. Only a couple of lamps were turned on. He stood at the window looking at the view.

She came up beside him, noting that he'd taken off his shoes, too.

"It's a far cry from where we each expected to be tonight," she commented. "You holding a new baby. Me enjoying a tropical evening."

"Regrets?"

She shook her head.

"Me, either."

"Are you a fatalist, Joe?"

"Yes," he said after a few seconds. "Even though

I strongly believe you determine your own path in life. Except when you don't."

She laughed softly. "Precisely."

They were being careful not to touch each other, she thought. *What next, Joe? Where do we go from here?*

"Should I order us something from room service?" he asked.

"Like what?"

"Dessert and coffee, maybe? Are you hungry?" When she didn't answer right away, he added, "There's apple pie with cinnamon ice cream on the menu, or chocolate fudge layer cake."

Her mouth watered, making her swallow. He angled closer. "You seem like a chocolate cake kind of woman."

"I would've called myself apple pie."

He shook his head slowly. "You're much more exotic than that."

Oh. Was he just feeding her a line? Were her instincts wrong? Maybe she needed to take a few steps back. "I have some granola bars in my carry-on…."

He eyed her for several long seconds, then he walked across the room to the nearest telephone and ordered two pieces of chocolate cake and a pot of decaf coffee. After he hung up he sat on the sofa and patted the cushion next to him. "Please."

Lauren perched there.

"I saw panic in your eyes," he said. "I don't need

conquests, Lauren. Bragging isn't part of who I am. Okay?"

"Okay."

"And anything that gets started can be stopped at any time. Just say the word."

"No?"

"Good night."

"That's two words."

He ran his fingertips down her hair, a feathery touch that yielded an explosion of reaction.

"What else do you have in your carry-on?" he asked. "What sorts of things did you come prepared for?"

"The usual necessities, in case my luggage didn't arrive at the same time."

"A deck of cards?"

"As a matter of fact, yes."

"Do you play poker?"

She crossed her arms automatically. "I'm not playing strip poker with you."

He laughed, a full, deep-throated sound of appreciation. "As appealing as that sounds, Ms. Wary, I was going to suggest we play carry-on poker."

"I've never heard of it."

"That's because I'm making it up as I go. Whoever loses the hand has to reveal an item from their carry-on."

"You must not have anything to hide."

"Maybe. Maybe I just don't expect to lose. Do you have something to hide?"

She had a couple of things that would be embarrassing for him to see, but she didn't plan on losing everything, either. "I might," she said. "The problem is that I figure you have a whole lot more stuff in yours, since it's twice the size of my bag and totally stuffed."

"That's the chance you have to take. You might have twenty little items, too. It's part of the game. The unknowns are exciting." He angled closer to her. "Are you a risk-taker, Lauren?"

She thought it over, acknowledged she wasn't at all a risk-taker, and decided it was time she changed that. "Okay, here's the deal," she said. "You have to take out all similar items at the same time, as one loss. If you have three shirts, that's considered one item. Deal?"

"What about toiletries? We had to pack most of them in one small plastic bag to get through security, but there could be a bunch of items. Does it count as one?"

She mentally tallied up the number she figured she had. They could drag out the game by counting every container individually, but did she want the game to drag out? She wanted time for...other things.

"Anything packaged together is considered one," she said.

"Works for me." He stood and headed toward the bedroom. "I'll get the bags."

Lauren was intrigued by the game, which might reveal more than conversation could. They couldn't hide behind any facade.

Her cell phone rang. She grabbed it off the coffee table and saw it was her son. She hadn't even said hello before he interrupted.

"Are you okay? You were supposed to call when you got to Nassau."

"There's a good reason why I didn't."

"There'd better be."

"I'm still in Chicago." She filled him in on most of the details. "How's the skiing?"

"Snowboarding. It's good. Except...Dad's being kind of a jerk."

Lauren said nothing. She didn't want to talk about Henry at all.

"I should've gone to the Bahamas with you," Jeremy said.

"Would've cramped my style, kid." She smiled at Joe as he set their bags on the floor at each end of the couch.

"Gimme a break, Mom. It's bad enough seeing Dad and Crystal all over each other. The thought of you... Yuk."

"Probably going to happen sometime, you know."

There was a knock on the door, then someone called out, "Room service."

"Living high?" Jeremy asked.

"I'm on vacation." She watched the server pull the cart to where Joe indicated. As soon as the employee left the room, Joe lifted a lid, grabbed one plate with an incredibly decadent looking piece of cake on it and ran it under her nose. Her mouth watered.

"Mom? Where'd you go? Are you getting the door or something?" Jeremy asked.

Lauren put a hand to her mouth as panic set in. How could she get out of this one? She fired a look at Joe, who raised his brows in question.

"You are alone, aren't you, Mom?"

"Of course I'm not alone," she said, infusing drama into her voice. "I picked up a gorgeous man at O'Hare, and we're sharing a suite at the Four Seasons, where the staff is amazingly quiet."

Jeremy laughed. "Stupid question, I guess. It's just that you sound a little different."

She watched Joe pour two cups of coffee. He pointed to the cream and sugar, and she nodded. "It's been a really long day."

"Okay, okay. Call me tomorrow and let me know what's going on."

"I promise. Thanks for checking on me. I love you."

"Love you, too."

"Jeremy," she said as she set the phone aside and picked up the cake.

"Apparently he didn't buy that you'd picked up a—gorgeous, did you say?—man and are spending the night with him."

"He laughed."

"If our children only knew that we are prudes only when it comes to *them*."

She lifted a bite of cake. "Exactly— Oh, my gosh, this is *good*." She closed her eyes and let the rich sweetness dissolve in her mouth. After a few seconds she opened her eyes and reached for her coffee, but stopped when she saw him just sitting and staring at her. She brushed her hand across her mouth, thinking she had crumbs on her face. "What?"

"Is that how you look when you climax?"

She swallowed. "There's never been a mirror on the bedroom ceiling."

Because he was still standing in front of her, she was eye level with his hips—

"Don't let my reaction scare you," he said, a little hoarsely. "Everything's under control."

He was just so darned *nice*, she thought. A gentleman. And yet one who was turned on by her, bigtime. She lifted her gaze before she did what she wanted to do—give in to the temptation and put her hand against his fly....

"If I was put together physically in the same way you are, Joe, you'd be seeing my reaction to you, too." There. Honesty. Because she'd only been kidding herself when she'd thought she didn't know where this evening would end. It would end in bed. In the meantime, a dull ache settled between her legs as she anticipated the buildup to them getting there.

He ran a finger along the skin revealed by the open V of her blouse, just a whisper of a touch, then he dipped his finger into her bra, hooking the catch and tugging her a little closer.

"Pink lace," he said. "I can just barely see it along the edges."

"Maybe strip poker, after all," she said, breathless.

He shook his head. "Let's play this out the way we started. There's time. Lots of time."

"You're a masochist. And a sadist."

"No. I'm a man wanting a beautiful woman, and wanting the moment to last."

"I don't know how long I can wait."

"Minute by minute, Lauren. No rules. No time-table. We're making a memory here." He dragged her bag next to her. "Cards?"

She unzipped the bag and found the cards in an inside pocket. While he shuffled them, she enjoyed her cake and coffee—and him. He was gorgeous, just as she'd told Jeremy, but not only on the outside. He was deep-down gorgeous, too.

They played the first hand. She won, her two pairs beating his one.

He dug into his bag and brought out a book, a thriller, exactly the kind of book she would've expected. His bookmark was inserted between pages 148 and 149. "Are you enjoying it?" she asked.

"Even better than his last."

"Are you a big reader?"

"I keep one going most of the time. You?" he asked.

"Yes, but just at night before I go to sleep. Otherwise I don't seem to have a lot of time these days."

She dealt the cards. This time she lost. She pulled out her own book, the same title as his. Her bookmark was between pages 208 and 209. They grinned at each other.

"Are you enjoying it?" he asked.

"Even better than his last. I need a distraction while I'm flying. I kept this book specifically for the flight."

"You must be a faster reader than I am." He dealt the cards.

"I probably just had more time." She lost again. She pulled out a turquoise one-piece bathing suit, cut high on the legs and low on top.

"No bikini? I'm disappointed."

"There's one in my suitcase, but just in case my luggage doesn't make it with me, this is the one I'd rather have."

"I didn't bring a bathing suit."

She smiled. "I can't imagine why not. Salt Lake City is such a hot spot this time of year."

He lost the next hand and pulled out a stack of T-shirts. "I can't open them and show you what's printed on them."

"Why not?" She reached for one as if she would snatch it away from him.

"They have my company logo on it. And my last name." He looked at her as if asking if she still wanted to keep up the no-last-name game. She hadn't changed her mind about that yet.

They played a few more hands. She learned he almost always wore jeans, and liked pullover V-neck sweaters. He learned she had to use a flatiron to get the kinks out of her hair. As they got to the bottoms of their bags, Lauren wondered what he had left. She would rather not pull out anything else. Did it matter to him?

He lost the next hand and brought out a stack of briefs.

"Ah. The eternal question answered," she said. "Not boxers."

"You prefer them?"

Her gaze drifted down him and back up. "I prefer none."

His jaw hardened, but he said nothing, just dealt

the cards. It was her turn to reveal her lingerie, new silk and lace items she'd bought for the trip, matching bras and panties in red and black.

He fingered the red panties, moved his hand over the silky fabric and along the crotch, slipping a finger inside.

She could almost feel him touching her. "Um, anything left in your bag of tricks?"

"Two things that probably count as one. How about you?"

"Also two things."

"You want to just show 'em?" he asked. "Or will you just hope you win and don't have to?"

"I'm game to empty the bags." *Get this over with and move on to whatever was next.* "You first."

He pulled out two hand-carved wooden cars.

"I made this one for Anna before she was born," he said, passing it to Lauren. She ran her fingers over the teeth marks on the well-loved toy.

"This is for Mariah." He handed over a brand-new car, newly carved and pristine.

"So you already had gifts. Buying the pretty outfit wasn't necessary."

"I liked that you helped me choose it. I'll remember that when I see her wearing it. And it'll surprise the heck out of Anna that I chose something like that." He ran his hands lovingly over the old car as he must've done a lot while he carved it. "Kids sure do grow up fast."

"Yes, they do." She passed the cars back to him and he tucked them away.

"I built a crib and changing table, too, and shipped it before Thanksgiving, then put them together there. I like that maybe they'll be used by future generations, long after I'm gone."

"That's wonderful."

"Now you," he said, moving his shoulders as if sloughing off memories.

She pulled out her bag of toiletries. He turned the bag over and over, looking at each item, as she had his earlier. Her birth control pills were visible. He didn't comment but the way he fingered the case said enough. Then he opened the bag and pulled out her travel-size bottle of perfume and sniffed it.

"Nice."

"It's a new fragrance for me."

He spritzed her neck then leaned close to her, breathing her scent, his nose brushing her skin. Her reaction came hard and fast. She wrapped her arms around his head, keeping him close. His tongue touched her neck, warm and wet and exciting. He dragged a slow, heated line to where he'd let his fingertips roam before, tracing the edge of fabric. A long, low sound came from her.

"Me, too," he breathed hot against her skin, then moved back slowly. "You have one more?"

She felt her face heat, but she reached into the bag and pulled out the last item.

CHAPTER 6

"A dozen condoms?" he said, laughter and surprise in his voice. "You expected to be busy in Nassau."

"There's a difference between expectation and being prepared." She set a hand on his. "I don't sleep around. I know you probably find it hard to believe, given the evidence in your hands and the fact that I'm here with you tonight—"

"Shh." He set the box like a glowing candle on the coffee table. "I never thought so. I don't, either. I haven't been intimate with anyone."

"I have, with one man, but I took every precaution."

"Okay. Good." He started putting his possessions back into his bag, so she did the same—except for the condoms.

"Would you mind if I take a shower?" he asked. "It's been a long day."

She figured he was being nice, giving her a chance to freshen up, too, knowing enough about women to know it was something she would want to do. "I wouldn't mind."

"I'll use the other shower then meet you back here. Don't rush."

They stood simultaneously, self-consciously. He smiled. "It's going to be all right, Lauren."

She nodded, but she'd had enough of the push/pull that had dominated the evening. Then he cupped her face and kissed her, and their mouths fit together in perfect alignment and harmony. He deepened the kiss, changing angles, need intensifying the sensations that rocketed through her. She dug her fingers into his waist as he slid his hands down her to cup her rear and pull her tightly to him. His shallow and unsteady breath matched hers. His tongue searched her mouth, sounds of pleasure reverberating down her throat. She buried her hands in his hair, pulling herself closer.

Finally he grabbed her arms and held her still, his chest heaving, his eyes dark and hungry.

"I'll hurry," she said, picking up her bag.

"Yeah." The word dragged along his throat.

She rushed the process, showering, adding perfume, dressing quickly. She debated wearing a robe then vetoed it. When she returned to the living room, only one lamp cast light in the space.

His hair damp, he waited a few feet from the bedroom door. He wore a hotel robe, and his eyes shone with approval of what she wore, a red silk-and-lace gown, cut daringly low, with spaghetti straps, and slits up the sides to midthigh.

He whistled, low and long. She felt…lusty. Happy to be a woman. Grateful her flight was canceled.

He took her in his arms then started dancing with her, slow and easy, molding their bodies, not covering much area.

"You look incredible," he said into her ear. "Feel incredible."

She nuzzled closer. "So do you."

"This is surreal, Lauren."

"Yes." She noticed the box was gone from the coffee table.

"On the nightstand in the bedroom."

Which meant he'd been in the bedroom while she showered and got ready. He'd been so close….

He bent to kiss her, and she gave herself up to him. They'd had all the important conversations they needed to. Now it was time to enjoy. To savor and luxuriate. They danced a little longer. She burrowed her face between the lapels of his robe and pressed her face to his chest, pushing the fabric aside as she tasted him, hearing his groans echo behind his ribs.

"I feel like a teenager," he said, low and rough. "This is going to be over too fast. Way too fast."

"Lucky for us, we have time for more than once."

Although time was dwindling fast, refusing to stand still as it should for such a momentous event. She stopped dancing and leaned back a little, resting her fingers on his robe sash, asking silent permission. He opened his arms. She untied the sash and let the robe fall open.

He was everything she'd expected and more. He wasn't just in good shape for his age, but in good shape, period. She grabbed the lapels and pushed slowly, giving him time to stop her. He let her shove the robe off him. It dropped onto their feet.

He closed his eyes and tipped back his head when she laid her hands flat against his chest and dragged them down, slowly, lightly until he sucked in air through his teeth.

"Not a good idea," he rasped, locking her wrists with his hands long enough to stop her, then reaching for the straps of her gown, sliding them down her arms, letting the weight of the fabric pull it to join his robe on the floor without a sound. He started dancing with her again, body to body, heat to heat, his hands moving over her, but restraint in his touch, too.

"I've never danced naked before," she said, barely aware of anything but him, the feel and taste of his skin, the wonder of his fingers teasing her.

"Try it doing the limbo."

She laughed quietly. "Have you?"

"No. But I'd like to watch you do it."

They were dancing only with their bodies now, not moving their feet, skin gliding against skin, hot and damp.

"I don't think I can wait another second," he said.

"Me, neither."

He surprised her by swooping her into his arms and carrying her into the bedroom, laying her on the bed, following her down. She opened to him, welcomed him. Then it all happened in an instant, the ascent peaking hard and fast, unyielding in intensity, unrelenting in satisfaction. It was far and away the best sex of her life. No getting-to-learn-what-you-like awkwardness, but a perfect merging, followed by the comforting feel of him blanketing her. Tears stung her eyes at the beauty of it all.

He rolled onto his side, taking her along, tucking her as close as he could, their legs entwining. He stroked her hair, held her tight, pressed his lips to her head. His breath came out shaky, emotion-filled.

"I would've like to have finessed that a little better," he said after a while.

"You finessed fine. But if you've got more in your repertoire, I'll be glad to let you show me."

They talked long into the night and made love again. He finessed the heck out of her, she told him, and she returned the favor. She must have dozed because suddenly he wasn't in bed beside her but standing at the bedroom window looking out at the city.

She slid out of bed, went to him and wrapped her arms around him from behind. "Everything okay?"

"Everything is beyond okay." He twisted so that she somehow ended up spooned in front of him, his arms enveloping her.

"Did I sleep long?" she asked.

"Nope."

"Did you want to be alone?"

"If I'd wanted that I would be in the living room."

"Anything you need to talk about?" she asked.

"Like what?"

"Whatever's on your mind."

"There's actually very little on my mind for the first time in recent memory. I feel like I'm on another planet."

"Is that good?"

"It's good."

She relaxed against him. "Tell me about the summer house you're building for yourself."

"It's lakefront property, and I'll build a deck with stairs down to a dock that will float on the water."

"Will you have a boat?"

"A canoe, for sure. Maybe a small fishing boat. The most noise you hear at the lake comes from the loons and very low horsepower outboard motors.

And occasional summer thunderstorms. Otherwise, it's incredibly quiet."

"Sounds relaxing." *Sounds heavenly.*

"That's what I'm counting on. A place to get away and make myself relax. It's big enough that kids and grandkids can come."

"One story?"

"Two. Four bedrooms, two baths. Big screened-in porch where we can eat and play games. I'm going to try not having a television."

"How much time do you think you'll spend there?"

"I'm shooting for every weekend during the summer." He rubbed his chin against her hair. "Do you think your son will come home every summer?"

"He hasn't decided. I think if he can find work in the area, he'll stay there."

"There's big competition for jobs for the college kids." He nuzzled her neck. "Could I interest you in a bath?"

"Together?"

"That would be the plan, yes."

"Sure." He headed toward the bathroom. Lauren continued to look out the window. A bath together. More memories to try to forget. How would any other relationship measure up to this one night of pure fantasy? Reality wouldn't have time to intrude. There wasn't anything about him she didn't like.

She was even totally comfortable naked with him, and that was a feat in itself.

She rubbed her forehead. Maybe she'd made a huge mistake, after all. Maybe regret would color her world forever.

"Headache?" he asked from behind her.

"No."

"Regrets?"

She turned around. "You'll be a hard act for someone to follow."

"If you knew all my annoying habits…"

She'd expected him to return the compliment, so she was speechless when he didn't. What did it mean? That she was making more of their night together than he was?

Well. Wasn't that what you said you wanted? One night without repercussions?

Yes, but.

But?

No buts. One night of pleasure. One night of wonder. He'd never implied more. And she'd promised herself only the one night, too.

"Lauren?"

She met his gaze.

"What's wrong?"

She shook her head. After a minute, he took her hand and they walked into the bathroom and climbed into the tub. After a lot of soaping up and teasing, they were laughing as water sloshed over the side. They dried each other off, sprawled on the huge bed and created one more memory.

She tried to stay awake after that, but as soon as he fell asleep, she gave in, too.

"Why didn't you wake me?"

Lauren caught Joe's reflection in the bathroom mirror as she finished fixing her hair. She was dressed and ready to go, would need to leave shortly to get to the airport on time.

"I figured one of us should actually get some sleep."

"I'm going to the airport with you."

She turned around as he approached. "No."

"Why not?"

"Your flight doesn't leave until five hours after mine. Just stay and get some sleep. You'll be busy when you get to Salt Lake."

He took her in his arms. "I can sleep in a chair or even on the floor after your flight leaves. I can sleep during my flight." His breath felt warm against her hair. "I can be ready to go in ten minutes."

"No." She laid her hands against his face. She would never forget him, but she needed to start trying. Right now.

"It's better this way, Joe." She'd spent the time she'd showered and dressed thinking about it, coming to the conclusion that she would fall apart at the airport. Bobbie had been right about them being in tender places. Lauren had been more susceptible to Joe's attention than she ever would have imagined. And despite what he said about being recovered, he was just now spreading his wings, even she could see that. He still had to soar some more before he would be ready to nest again. A long-distance relationship would have little chance to succeed. She was the first woman he'd made love to since his wife died. Of course he would have particularly warm thoughts for Lauren.

And if he'd said anything during the night to make her think things might go further with them, she might have reconsidered—but he hadn't. He could have invited her to call him when she visited her son at college, but he hadn't suggested it. He even could have proposed the possibility that Jeremy might get a summer job on his crew. He hadn't.

So now she had to be a woman of her word and just move on.

He took a few steps back and crossed his arms. "Did you call to see if your flight's on time?"

"Yes, and it is. Joe? This has been the best night of my life."

He softened. "Then why—"

"Please. Can we leave it like this?"

Silence buzzed in the room. He opened his arms, and she walked into them.

"I'm very glad we met," he said against her hair.

"Me, too. Have a wonderful time with your family."

"I will. Don't get too sunburned."

Their goodbye kiss started out soft and tender and escalated in a hurry, as perfect as a farewell kiss could be.

"Goodbye, Joe," she said against his lips.

"Take care."

Lauren grabbed her carry-on and made herself walk out of the room without looking back, even though she knew he was watching her.

O'HARE WAS a hive of activity as the airlines tried to make up for the cancellations of the day before. Lauren didn't find an empty chair before her flight was announced, and so she wandered instead.

When her flight was called for boarding, she made her way to the gate, waited for her row to be called, then got in line. She made idle chat with the woman in front of her, who'd also spent the night in Chicago. Lauren welcomed the distraction to the fireball sitting in the middle of her chest, waiting for a private moment to be released.

Her divorce had devastated her, but she'd had hurt and anger to keep her company then. Now she just had what-ifs, and an incredible memory that wouldn't die anytime soon.

But she'd done the right thing by not sharing last

names and leaving on her own this morning. She was positive of that. He wasn't ready for a relationship, and he would certainly come to that realization by himself after a little bit of time passed.

She slid her carry-on along and had almost made it to the gate attendant's stand when she thought she heard her name being called. She looked around… and spotted Joe, holding a cardboard sign over his head with a phone number scrawled on it.

He didn't say anything. Didn't smile. In fact, he looked so solemn she almost stepped out of the line and went to offer him comfort, anything to put a smile back on his face.

"Ma'am? Your boarding pass, please?"

Startled, she handed it to the young man.

"Have a nice flight."

She took small, hesitant steps, other people passing her by. She looked at Joe's face again, registered the sadness, then walked into the long, cavernous, lonely Jetway.

CHAPTER 7

"I screwed up," Lauren said, cupping a huge bowl-shaped glass full to the brim. "You warned me. I warned myself. And still I let it happen."

"Let what happen?" Bobbie asked, looking off into the distance.

"What have we been talking about for the past three hours? *Him*. Joe. One night of wonder." She opened her arms. "Look at me. I'm a mess. This trip was supposed to be fun, and here it is, the first night and I'm crying in my margarita. Aren't you glad you came?" she asked sarcastically.

The setting sun created a spectacular pink-and-orange sky amid billowing clouds, the temperature still hovering around seventy. People ringed a huge, sparkling pool, lounging in chairs, talking and laughing, being served colorful tropical drinks. A man standing at the bar across the pool waved at Bobbie. She waved back.

"Yes, I'm glad I came," Bobbie said. "And you

need to snap out of it. Joe obviously wants to continue the relationship. What's wrong with that?"

"He's not *ready*."

"So *you* say. Maybe he thinks otherwise."

"Well, what am I supposed to do? He lives over a
thousand miles away. I'd spend time and money only
to delay inevitable heartbreak."

"It sounds like he wants to try it." Bobbie sat up
straighter and finger-combed her hair. "Maybe *you*
want to spend the week moping, but I'm going to
have fun. Jim's headed this way. You can stay long
enough to be introduced, then you need to find a
reason to go away."

Lauren watched the striking steel-haired man walk
toward them, his khakis and flowered shirt looking
freshly pressed. Bobbie had met him the night before
at the bar, and they'd talked until two o'clock in the
morning. He'd been out on a fishing expedition all
day or they probably would've spent the day together.

Jim sat at the bottom of Bobbie's lounge and was
introduced. "So, you made it," he said to Lauren.
"No other delays?"

"No problems at all. How was the fishing?"

"Productive. I'm having the chef prepare the
catch for dinner." He looked at Bobbie. "I hope
you'll join me. Your sister, too, of course."

Bobbie narrowed her eyes at Lauren. She knew
that look. Had known it for forty-five years.

"I appreciate the invitation," Lauren said, "but I'm pretty wiped out after the stress of the past couple of days. I was planning on going to bed early."

"You have to eat."

Lauren waited a moment for Bobbie to chime in. She didn't. She'd never seen her sister like this. Maybe that was why she was encouraging Lauren toward Joe. Maybe she'd discovered love at first sight.

"Thanks, but no," Lauren said, knowing her role, but curious about him. "I wouldn't be great company. Are you here alone?" she asked, ignoring her sister's heat-seeking-missile stare.

"No, my children and grandchildren are with me. We've made it our Christmas tradition for four years now. Since my wife passed away."

Ah, widowed, like Bobbie. It gave them something in common to start with. "Where do you live?"

"Savannah."

About ninety miles from Charleston, where Bobbie lived. Not too inconvenient.

"I'm an attorney, criminal law," he said, winking at Bobbie, obviously understanding he was being grilled and instead offering answers to potential questions. "I'm fifty-nine. Don't plan to retire for about three more years. Still have all my teeth. Cholesterol's a little high but I'm working on it. Blood pressure is good, which is amazing in my occupation. Don't need Viagra."

Lauren laughed as Bobbie's face flushed pink, beyond what two days in the sun had put there.

"Satisfied?" she asked Lauren.

"Are you going to break my sister's heart?" Lauren asked Jim.

"I'm more worried about her breaking mine," he said, taking Bobbie's hand.

Time to give them space, Lauren decided. She'd embarrassed Bobbie enough.

"I'll try not to monopolize her," Jim said as Lauren stood to leave. "I know you'll want time together."

"I have a feeling I'm going to be catching up on my reading this week." She hugged her sister, happy for her. "Have fun."

In her room, Lauren unpacked, having put off the task to lounge by the pool instead after she'd arrived. She held the red nightgown to her face for a moment then stuffed it in her suitcase. The box of condoms wouldn't be necessary, either, so she tossed them in there as well, locking in the memories.

She ordered room service and sat on her balcony until she couldn't stand being idle a moment longer. Tired, but knowing she wouldn't sleep yet, she headed downstairs, not willing to wallow by herself in the room all night.

Wearing her sarong as a shawl, she made her way to the beach, carrying her sandals as she walked along the shore, letting the low waves almost reach her before jogging a few steps away, getting caught once by surprise. The wet hem of her dress clung to her after that. A mild breeze blew her hair. It would be perfect if she had someone to share it with.

She thought back to her life with Henry, the vacations they'd taken, mostly ones to visit family, hers or his, rarely anyplace where they'd stayed in a hotel, and certainly nothing tropical. He didn't like sand.

And yet, he and Crystal took nice vacations now. Maybe Crystal demanded it.

Lauren could see what Henry saw in his young wife. Aside from being flattered by her youth, she was very feminine and doting, letting him be the boss. He would like that a lot.

Lauren returned to the hotel and found a chair by the wall overlooking the beach.

"Would you like something from the bar?" one of the studly—as Bobbie had called them—pool boys asked.

She looked directly at him, but all she saw was Joe's phone number in red neon on his forehead.

"I, um, yes. Coffee, please. With cream and sugar."

"I'll be back shortly."

"Oh, wait a second. Do you have chocolate cake?"

"We do."

"A piece of that, too, please."

He nodded and left.

She wondered what Joe was doing. Was he holding his granddaughter? Laughing with his children?

Getting over her?

She could've called him at any point during the day. He'd left it entirely in her hands. How long until he decided she wouldn't be making that call?

The server brought her coffee and cake. She took a bite. Good, but not nirvana like last night's.

Okay, she thought, sitting up, trying to clear her mind. She had options. She could wallow all week or she could enjoy herself. It was foolish to pay so much money to come to this beautiful resort and not have a good time. Plus, she didn't want to bring Bobbie down, either, although maybe they wouldn't end up seeing that much of each other.

"That looks good," a man said from beside her.

She set down her fork as he grabbed the chair next to hers, sliding it over a little, but not sitting.

"It's not bad," she said.

"Not a strong recommendation. Hi, I'm Conrad." He was probably fifteen years older than she. He had a full head of white hair, slicked back with some kind of gel or something. Not one strand moved in the breeze. "Would you mind having company?"

Yes. "I was about to head to my room, actually."

"Not until you finish your dessert, though, right?"

Tears pushed at her eyes. She set her plate next

to her untasted coffee on a side table. "I'm sorry. I have to go."

She left him there.

Tomorrow, she promised herself. Tomorrow she would start having fun and not be a downer for Bobbie. Right now she needed to wallow. Just for tonight.

CHAPTER 8

"Offer still stands," Jim said to Lauren as she waited in her room for the bellman to pick up her suitcases.

"I appreciate it. I really do. But my son will be home New Year's Day, and I haven't seen him in months." Jim's offer to fly her home on his chartered jet was tempting, but it would mean staying four extra days, and she didn't want to do that. Plus she was ready to get away from Bobbie and Jim's adoring absorption in each other.

Lauren had survived Christmas, after all. More than survived. Her entire attitude about the holiday had changed in Chicago, and she didn't let it slip back to the old one again, would never bah-humbug the holiday again. The resort staff had gone all out to make Christmas away from home a good one for the guests, and she'd enjoyed herself. She'd been surrounded by family, such as it was—Bobbie and Jim's group, a big, fun-loving crowd.

"I'll leave you two to say your goodbyes, then,"

Jim said, giving Lauren a hug. "I'm sorry I hogged your sister's attention."

"No, you're not."

He grinned. "Guilty as charged." He sent a tender look Bobbie's way then left the room.

"The man is besotted," Lauren said to Bobbie.

"He's not alone."

She took Bobbie's hand, pulled her to sit beside her on one of the beds. "You think he's the one, sis?"

"Yes."

Lauren was bothered by the relationship. She couldn't put her finger on why exactly, but she acknowledged that as the week passed, she'd grown more uncomfortable with it. "How can you know so fast, Bobbie?"

"Some things just make sense. I've dated quite a bit, as you know. I've been infatuated before. This is different."

"He also comes with kids and grandkids."

"Isn't it wonderful? I had a good life with John, and not having children was something I was resigned to. But Jim has four children. Seven grandchildren, so far. It's my idea of heaven."

"Well, you are glowing."

Then her big sister, who so rarely got emotional about anything, burst into tears. "Oh, Lauren. I'm so in love with him."

Lauren took her into her arms, stunned at

Bobbie's outburst. "He loves you, too. It's written all over his face."

"He makes me feel so sexy," she whispered.

Lauren laughed as Bobbie pulled back and wiped her fingers across her damp cheeks.

"Well, he *does*."

"That's very important."

"What are you going to do about the man who made *you* feel so sexy?" Bobbie asked.

"Cherish the memory. I don't know how to say it any differently from the twenty other times this week I've said it—he's not ready. I'm sure that since I haven't contacted him all week, he's already given up."

"But—"

"No more." Lauren stood. "I had a great time, even though I didn't see you tons. You can thank me anytime now for my flight being delayed, thus giving you the opportunity to meet Jim."

"Thank you. But we would've met regardless, I'm sure of it. Obviously with all his family here, he wasn't looking to hook up, but he says it would've ended up the same."

"Okay then. You can thank me for convincing you to join me here for Christmas."

"Actually," Bobbie said, a twinkle in her eyes, "I think we should be thanking Henry. He started it all."

They both held up imaginary glasses and shouted, "To Henry."

They smiled at each other then hugged, long and hard. "How nice to know you have a date for New Year's Eve tomorrow," Lauren said, the thought stinging a little.

"You could, too, I think."

"Stop," Lauren said, laughing, exasperated. "You're relentless."

A knock on the door ended their conversation as the bellman appeared and took away her bags. She didn't relish the twelve or thirteen hours of travel ahead of her and hoped she didn't get delayed again.

She just wanted to get home.

"Goodbye, sweet sister," she said to Bobbie. "Be happy."

"I am."

On the first leg of her flight home, Lauren stewed. Should she have said something to her sister about her concerns? Since she didn't know exactly what was bothering her about Jim, what could she have said? And wouldn't Bobbie have just been angry at Lauren for interfering instead of just being happy for her?

Then on the second leg, Lauren finally put her finger on it.

She was jealous.

She wasn't worried about Jim breaking Bobbie's heart. No. Lauren was envious, and looking for reasons not to like him, not to believe he could also fall in love with Bobbie so fast. Because that would justify Lauren's rationale that she hadn't fallen for Joe that fast, either.

And she *had* fallen. Hard.

Logic dictated how slim the chances were of her ending up with Joe. And yet she wanted to try. She wanted to be as happy as Bobbie.

Even if just for a while.

She'd recovered from a divorce, and that was hard and painful. She could recover from Joe, too, if she had to. But she didn't have to, not yet.

Unless he'd changed his mind in the past week.

Anticipation grabbed her as she deplaned in Chicago. She only had an hour until her flight to Cedar Rapids, and she knew she should find her new gate first and make sure it was on schedule, but she couldn't wait.

She was barely out of the Jetway when she dialed the number burned into her brain. It rang. Rang again. Again.

"Hello?"

Her heart slammed into her sternum at the sound of his voice.

"Joe?"

"Hello, Four Seasons."

Oh, he sounded wonderful, and happy to hear from her.

"I didn't wait too long, did I?" she asked.

"Too long for what?"

"To call. To tell you I—I want to see you again."

"Turn around."

The crowd noise had her pressing the phone closer. She'd obviously misheard him. "What did you say?"

"Turn around."

She did. And he was there, in front of her, smiling.

"You're—" she realized she didn't need the phone, and snapped it shut "—here. How did you manage that?"

"I knew the day you were supposed to come back. I had to work my flight for the same day, since I wouldn't be allowed in the boarding area unless I had a ticket. I've been waiting for six hours."

"You were willing to take a chance—"

He hauled her into his arms and kissed her, holding on tight, not caring that they blocked traffic, as other passengers bumped into them.

"I missed you," he said roughly when he swallowed her up in his arms. "I thought about you every minute of every day."

"How did you know I'd want to see you, too?"

"You just needed a little time to process your feelings."

She leaned back so that she could see his face.

"What if I'd changed my flight? What if I hadn't come through O'Hare for some reason?"

He brushed her hair from her face with gentle fingertips. "Apparently you didn't use any condoms this week."

After what they'd shared? "Of course not. Why?"

"I slipped my business card into the box. You would've found it eventually, I figured."

"Probably not for a long time."

He smiled. "I had an ace in the hole." He glanced at her carry-on bag sitting at her feet. "I looked at your luggage tag. I know where you live."

"And you would've come after me?"

"Like Sherman marching to Atlanta. So, Ms. Lauren Wright, my name is Joe Mancini, and I'd like to know what you're doing New Year's Eve."

She rested her cheek against his shoulder, blinking back tears. "I think I have a date with a tall, dark and handsome builder from Maine."

"That, you do."

Jeremy would have to understand if she wasn't home for a couple of days. He had his whole winter break ahead of him.

But she was just starting her life.

* * * * *

*Be sure to return to Next in January
for more entertaining women's fiction
about the next passion in a woman's life.
For a sneak preview of* Risky Business
*by Merline Lovelace,
coming to Next in January,
please turn the page.*

Sue Ellen Carson was girded for battle when Joe Goodwin arrived later that afternoon.

She'd met the man on several previous occasions, once at her friend Andi's bookstore and once to try to resolve the issue of Phase One. At Andi's store he'd been in jeans and a T-shirt that stretched tight across rippling pecs and laser-incised lats. On the second occasion he'd dressed for their meetings in the standard Florida business attire of slacks and an open-necked short-sleeved shirt.

When Goodwin strode into her office at precisely 5:01 p.m., he was still in his military uniform. His maroon beret sat low on his forehead. His sand-hued desert BDUs bristled with subdued insignia and patches that Sue Ellen guessed meant he could infiltrate any remote patch on the globe by air, sea or camel. The rack of stripes on each sleeve spoke for themselves. She knew no one achieved the rank of chief master sergeant in the elite Special Ops community unless they were tougher than kryptonite and meaner than barbed wire.

He wasn't the only one in the room with a steel backbone, however. Despite her scant inches, pansy-purple eyes and preference for ankle bracelets and strappy sandals over lace-up combat boots, Sue Ellen hadn't reached *her* position by rolling over and playing dead when confronted with very large, very intimidating males. Lifting her chin, she issued a cool greeting.

"Chief."

"Ms. Carson."

He dragged off his beret and stuffed it into the leg pocket of his BDUs. Removing that symbol of lethal power didn't do much to soften his image. Skin tanned to leather and salt-and-pepper hair shaved so close to the scalp as to make him appear almost bald still sent distinct, don't-mess-with-me signals.

"Have a seat."

She waved him to one of the chairs in front of her desk, in no mood to offer more casual seating at the round conference table in the corner of her office. Nor did she intend to give him the edge by admitting she'd been railroaded into attending his damned camp. Let him drag it out of her.

"I understand we need to talk about STEP," she said, still cool, still polite.

"We do. Before we get started, you might want to take a look at these."

He delved into the pocket on his other pant leg and produced a folded manila envelope. From that he extracted several documents.

"This gives the name and background information on the teen you'll be paired with during survival training. Her name is Rose Gutierrez. Rose has had a tough time," the chief continued. "STEP is her last stop before a juvenile detention center."

Sue Ellen didn't like the sound of that. Frowning, she glanced at the papers with a frisson of alarm. Who had Goodwin paired her with? And what exactly did "pairing" entail, anyway? Before she could ask, his gaze locked with hers. All trace of a smile had disappeared from his eyes.

"That's why I wanted to see you this afternoon."

"To warn me about Rose?"

"To let you take out your anger at being coerced into this on me, so you don't take it out on her."

Sue Ellen sucked in a swift breath. Not only had the man gone over her head, he had the unmitigated gall to sit there and suggest she would actually put their private differences ahead of an adolescent's welfare.

"I was angry before," she said, her eyes narrowed to slits. "Now I'm *pissed off*."

JOE FELT THE IMPACT of that dagger glare right down to his boot tops. He'd racked up twenty-six years in uniform, most of them in Special Ops. During those years he'd honed his instincts to a razor's edge—and every one of them was now shouting that he'd just made a serious tactical error.

Until this point he'd held two competing but not necessarily contradictory opinions of Ms. Sue Ellen Carson. First, she was all woman. Her feathery blond hair, heart-shaped face and deep purple eyes came packaged with a seductive set of curves that could make a man trip over his own tongue. Second, she was a bureaucratic, bullheaded pain in the ass.

Viewing her now, with those amethyst eyes flashing and fury staining her cheeks, Joe amended his opinion to include a third view. The stubborn, delectable Ms. Carson was no lightweight. She looked ready to bite into him, chew him up and spit him out right then and there.

Joe didn't get that kind of ferocity from many men, let alone a slip of a female who wouldn't come up to his chin without the ankle-busting spike heels she was wearing. Thinking of her footwear reminded him of the second reason he'd driven all the way over to Pensacola for this face-to-face.

"I'll do my best to get you unpissed off in the next three weeks," he promised. "But first, you'd better make a quick trip to a camping or outdoor recreation supply shop. All you're encouraged to bring… Correction, all you're allowed to bring are the personal items on that list and any prescribed medications. Oh, and a good supply of bug spray."

With what sounded like a strangled groan, she reached for the envelope he'd put on her desk and slid out the camp brochure. Joe figured he'd better make his getaway before she skimmed the extremely abbreviated list of approved personal items. He had a feeling the elegant Ms. Carson was *not* going to be thrilled about having to wash her undies in swamp water every night.

"Call me if you have any questions." Tugging his beret from his leg pocket, he rose. "I included my home and cell phone numbers in the packet."

He almost made it to the door. A sharp exclamation brought him around.

"Goodwin!"

"Yeah?"

"I don't go anywhere without a cell phone." She rose to her feet and planted her hands on the desk. Both her voice and expression telegraphed a flat refusal to compromise. "It's a matter of safety, not convenience."

They'd reached their first critical make-or-break point and they hadn't even taken to the field yet. Joe knew he had to win this one or forget trying to convince her of the value of his program.

"That's the whole point of Phase One," he said evenly. "Teaching participants to rely on themselves, not mechanical devices that could fail or might not be available in a crisis situation. Try it for the first week my way. If that doesn't work, we'll reassess the situation. Deal?"

He thought for a moment she was going to refuse. Her mouth opened. Shut with a snap. Finally she dipped her head in a curt nod.

"Deal."

Silhouette®
Desire

When Kimberley Blackstone's father is
presumed dead, Kimberley is required to take
over the helm of Blackstone Diamonds. She
has to work closely with her ex, Ric Perrini, to
battle not only the press, but also the fierce
attraction still sizzling between them. Does Ric
feel the same...or is it the power her share of
Blackstone Diamonds will provide him as he
battles for boardroom supremacy.

Look for

VOWS &
A VENGEFUL GROOM

by

BRONWYN
JAMESON

Available January wherever you buy books

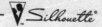

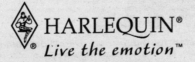

REQUEST YOUR FREE BOOKS!

2 FREE NOVELS PLUS 2 FREE GIFTS!

N^e_xt ™

There's the life you planned. And there's what comes next.

YES! Please send me 2 FREE Harlequin® NEXT™ novels and my 2 FREE mystery gifts. After receiving them, if I don't wish to receive any more books, I can return the shipping statement marked "cancel." If I don't cancel, I will receive 4 brand-new novels every other month and be billed just $3.99 per book in the U.S. or $4.74 per book in Canada, plus 25¢ shipping and handling per book plus applicable taxes, if any.* That's a savings of over 25% off the cover price! I understand that accepting the 2 free books and gifts places me under no obligation to buy anything. I can always return a shipment and cancel at any time. Even if I never buy anything from Harlequin, the two free books and gifts are mine to keep forever.   155 HDN EL33 355 HDN EL4F

Name _____ (PLEASE PRINT)

Address _____ Apt. #_____

City _____ State/Prov. _____ Zip/Postal Code _____

Signature (if under 18, a parent or guardian must sign)

Order online at www.TryNEXTNovels.com

Or mail to the **Harlequin Reader Service®:**

IN U.S.A.: P.O. Box 1867, Buffalo, NY 14240-1867
IN CANADA: P.O. Box 609, Fort Erie, Ontario L2A 5X3

Not valid to current Harlequin NEXT subscribers.

Want to try two free books from another line?
Call 1-800-873-8635 or visit www.morefreebooks.com

* Terms and prices subject to change without notice. NY residents add applicable sales tax. Canadian residents will be charged applicable provincial taxes and GST. This offer is limited to one order per household. All orders subject to approval. Credit or debit balances in a customer's account(s) may be offset by any other outstanding balance owed by or to the customer. Please allow 4 to 6 weeks for delivery.

Your Privacy: Harlequin Books is committed to protecting your privacy. Our Privacy Policy is available online at www.eHarlequin.com or upon request from the Harlequin Reader Service. From time to time we make our lists of customers available to reputable firms who may have a product or service of interest to you. If you would prefer we not share your name and address, please check here. ☐

NEXT07R

ATHENA FORCE

Heart-pounding romance and thrilling adventure.

CAUGHT IN THE CROSS FIRE

Francesca Thorn is the FBI's best profiler...and she's needed to target Athena Academy's most dangerous foe. But as she gets dangerously close to revealing the identity of her alma mater's greatest threat, someone will stop at nothing to ensure she remains dead silent. Her only choice is to accept all the help her irritatingly sexy U.S. Army bodyguard can provide.

ATHENA FORCE

Will the women of Athena unravel Arachne's powerful web of blackmail and death...or succumb to their enemies' deadly secrets?

Look for

MOVING TARGET

by *Lori A. May,*

Executive Sue Ellen Carson was ordered by her boss to undergo three weeks of wilderness training run by retired USAF officer Joe Goodwin. She was there to evaluate the program for federal funding approval. But trading in power suits for combat fatigues was hard enough—fighting off her feelings for Joe was almost impossible....

Look for

RISKY BUSINESS

by

MERLINE LOVELACE

Available January wherever you buy books

The Next Novel.com

HARLEQUIN®

N**e**xt™

HN88149

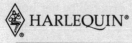

COMING NEXT MONTH

#99 RISKY BUSINESS • Merline Lovelace
For executive Sue Ellen Carson, approving or denying
funding for a camp for troubled teens is just another thing
to check off the to-do list from the comfort of her air-
conditioned office. Until her boss orders her to undergo
three weeks of wilderness training run by retired USAF
officer Joe Goodwin. Trading in power suits for combat
fatigues is hard enough—fighting off her feelings for Joe
is almost impossible....

**#100 MOTHERHOOD WITHOUT WARNING •
Tanya Michaels**
Della Carlisle has hit her stride with a great career, a
fantastic love life with a younger man, the works. But
one pregnancy test changes everything. The idea of having
Alexander DiRossi's baby and becoming his traditional
little housewife sends chills down Della's spine. It takes
her friends who have been there, done that, to make her
see that motherhood isn't the end of the fun—it's the
beginning!